STARBORN

FLAME AND CATALYST

JOHN KNIGHT

TABLE OF CONTENTS

CHAPTER ONE: STRANGERS IN THE DUST

The twin suns of Nytharis hung low in the sky, turning the canyon into a furnace of shadow and gold. Heat shimmered off the cracked earth. Dust swirled in restless spirals, carrying the scent of rust, scorched stone, and the faint tang of ozone. To most, this world was dead; a forgotten backwater with nothing but ghosts and sand. But to Calen Rourke, it was something else.

It was calling to him.

Kneeling beside a jagged outcrop, Calen adjusted the cracked filter mask over his face and swept the stone surface with his handheld scanner. The readings were erratic again—sharp magnetic flares, microbursts of unknown energy, and faint radiation spikes that defied explanation. The same pattern he'd been chasing across Nytharis for over two weeks.

"Another anomaly," he muttered. "Third one today."

He tapped his wristband, tagging the coordinates. As he brushed aside a layer of sand, he uncovered smooth, unnatural metal—curved, etched faintly, buried under centuries of dust. Not debris. Not Concord tech. Something older. Forgotten.

Not for the first time, Calen wondered what he was really doing here.

He'd told the syndicate he was on survey duty, scanning for rare-earth mineral veins and salvage-worthy wreckage. But that was the cover. The truth was more complicated—and more personal.

He had come to Nytharis because of a dream.

Not once, but over and over, for the last year. Always the same. A canyon bathed in twin light. A woman with silver eyes standing in the wind. And a single word, echoing through the dark: *Zephyra.*

He had no reason to know that name. No memory of its meaning. But it had haunted him, stitched itself into his mind like a song he couldn't stop humming. He'd chased fragments—star maps, corrupted transmissions, Concord black files. All led him here.

Something was buried beneath this planet. He could feel it.

And it was waking.

A low hum shivered through the ground, vibrating through his boots.

Calen froze.

Not tectonic activity. Not wind.

Then came the sharp slap of footsteps.

He turned just as a figure darted into view from the ridge—fast, agile, silhouetted against the glaring suns. A woman. Her pale blue skin glistened with sweat, and her white hair streamed behind her like a comet's tail. Her gear was torn, dusty, clinging to a frame built for survival. In one hand, she gripped a glowing blade.

Behind her, something screamed.

A combat drone shot into view—sleek, black, deadly. Its red optics locked on the fleeing woman, targeting beams slicing through the air.

Calen moved on instinct.

He dropped to one knee, flipped his rifle off his back, and fired. The pulse round hit the drone dead centre. It sparked, spun, and crashed into the rocks with a screeching metallic howl.

The woman staggered to a stop, blade raised—but not toward the drone. Toward him.

Her eyes fixed on him—silver and brilliant, wary as a cornered cat. "Who are you?"

He lowered his rifle slowly. "That drone was about to vaporize you. You're welcome."

She didn't blink. Her voice was melodic but sharp. "They found me."

"They?"

"The Iron Rebellion."

His brow furrowed. "You make a habit of angering planetary-scale death cults, or is today special?"

She nearly collapsed then, knees buckling. She caught herself on a jagged rock, clutching her side.

Calen stepped forward, cautiously. "You're hurt."

"I can manage."

"Sure doesn't look like it."

He reached into his satchel, pulling out a water vial and a field patch. She didn't move.

"Name's Calen," he offered. "Calen Rourke. I'm not with your enemies. Just a scavenger. Here mapping anomalies."

Her silver eyes scanned him, reading his stance, his worn gear, the lack of insignia.

Finally, she straightened. "Aelira. Princess Aelira Vaelori. Of Zephyra."

Calen blinked. The name hit him like a blow to the chest.

Zephyra.

The word from his dreams. The place that haunted him.

He kept his face neutral. "Royalty? On this dump of a planet? Either you're very lost or very unlucky."

"Both. And they'll be back. That drone was just a scout."

He looked up toward the distant ridge, where dust was already beginning to stir again.

"There's a ravine nearby," he said. "Two klicks north. Shielded on three sides. I use it for shelter."

"You'd risk it? For a stranger?"

He met her gaze. "You're not a stranger anymore. And something tells me... you're the reason I'm here."

She hesitated—not long, but enough to measure the weight of his words.

Then she nodded. "Lead the way, Rourke."

They turned together and ran into the falling light, shadows stretching long behind them as the triple moons began to rise.

And high above, veiled behind storm-swept clouds, a rebel vessel adjusted course.

The hunt had begun.

CHAPTER TWO: ECHOES BENEATH THE STONE

The ravine narrowed as they descended, its steep walls rising like jagged ribs of some fossilized titan. Calen moved ahead, scanning each ledge with his wristband, guiding Aelira with short, steady nods. Loose shale crunched beneath their boots. Every sound seemed louder here, trapped between stone walls that swallowed the wind.

"This way," Calen murmured. "There's a hollow I marked last time I passed through. Shielded on 6three sides by natural overhang. Good cover. Even if they send aerials."

Aelira moved with careful grace behind him. Despite her wound, she made almost no sound. But Calen noticed the way her breath hitched, how her left hand never left her ribs. She was pushing through pain — and pride.

He paused at a steep drop. "Need a hand?"

"I'm fine."

"You keep saying that." He reached down anyway.

She hesitated, then took it.

Her fingers were cold. Calloused. Stronger than they looked. He helped her down without comment, letting the contact linger just a second longer than necessary.

They moved in silence until the ravine opened into a half-collapsed cavern — a jagged wound in the canyon wall. Light spilled in through a narrow gap in the ceiling, illuminating shards of broken stone and dry moss. One wall curved unnaturally smooth, as if melted by time or fire.

Calen swept his scanner across the interior. "No heat signatures. No power spikes. We're alone. For now."

Aelira exhaled slowly and eased herself down against a boulder. Dust clung to her skin. Her blade lay across her knees, dim now — as if sleeping.

Calen knelt and pulled a protein bar from his pack, tossing it to her. Then a water capsule. Then a Medistrip. "Use it."

She caught the bar, eyed it suspiciously, then gave a nod of thanks. "You're well-prepared."

"Occupational hazard. I don't like surprises."

"Too late for that."

He offered a small smile. "Fair point."

She reached into a satchel at her side and pulled out a crystalline shard the size of a coin. It shimmered faintly, pale blue and pulsing. She pressed it to her side. The light spread out in gentle lines across her skin, knitting tissue, cooling the burn.

Calen watched, impressed. "Zephyrian meditech?"

She nodded. "Heirloom. From my mother."

He tilted his head. "You don't talk like a princess."

"Good. I stopped being one the day the palace burned."

The silence stretched.

"I'm sorry," Calen said.

She glanced at him. "You don't even know what happened."

"I know loss. That's enough."

Something shifted in her gaze. A wall softened — slightly.

Then his scanner pulsed. A slow, rhythmic blink.

He frowned and tapped the side. "That's new."

Aelira sat up straighter. "What is it?"

He adjusted the display. "Faint signal. Magnetic frequency. Very low-level. Below us."

Her eyes narrowed. "Buried tech?"

"Or something older."

She stood, wincing. "Show me."

He led her to the back wall — the smooth one. He placed his palm against it. Warm. Not from the sun.

The scanner blinked again — in perfect rhythm. Then stopped.

"I think this wall is listening," Calen said quietly.

Aelira stepped beside him, blade in hand. "To what?"

"To us."

And behind the stone, something pulsed once... and waited.

CHAPTER THREE: THE VAULT BELOW

The wall shivered beneath Calen's palm.

Aelira stepped closer, her eyes locked on the smooth, faintly glowing surface. "It's reacting."

"Not just to me," Calen said. "To both of us."

Without warning, a symbol bloomed beneath his hand — a circle intersected by two radiant lines. The same shape that haunted his dreams. It pulsed once... then split.

Stone that should have been solid flowed like mist. A seam cracked open, revealing a narrow archway bathed in pale blue light. Dust drifted like snow in the still air beyond.

Calen lifted his rifle, heart pounding. "Well... you first, Princess."

Aelira didn't smile. But she walked past him without hesitation, blade in hand, shoulders squared.

They stepped into the hidden chamber together.

It was vast — far larger than the exterior suggested. Hexagonal panels lined the curved walls, etched with fine circuitry that pulsed gently like veins of living metal. Thin conduits reached from floor to ceiling, their glow soft but constant. The room smelled faintly of ozone and something older — dry, metallic, preserved.

At the centre, a pedestal stood beneath a shaft of light. Upon it, a metallic sphere hovered — smooth, perfect, spinning slowly as if weightless. Rings of symbols turned around it, shifting in sequence like a language just out of reach.

Calen stepped closer, eyes wide. "This isn't Concord tech."

Aelira circled it warily. "It's Zephyrian."

"No," he said softly. "Older."

She frowned. "How would you know?"

He didn't answer right away. He just stared at the sphere — the way it moved, the way the light curved around it. His chest ached suddenly, not with pain, but familiarity.

"I've seen this before," he murmured. "In the dream."

Aelira's eyes sharpened. "The one that brought you here?"

He nodded. "There was a tower... and this. Hovering. Waiting."

She looked between him and the artifact. "This isn't coincidence."

The sphere's glow intensified.

Then a voice — soft, layered — filled the chamber. Not through sound, but inside their minds.

"Two flames. One spark. The Catalyst returns."

Calen staggered back. Aelira pressed a hand to her temple.

"What the hell was that?" he breathed.

Aelira's eyes flicked toward the pedestal. "A guardian? An imprint?"

The air shimmered again. Lines of energy reached out from the sphere, weaving in the space between them like strands of light — connecting Calen and Aelira in a halo of flickering flame.

"Get back," she said sharply.

"I'm not doing this," Calen replied.

The light wrapped tighter, pulsing with a rhythm not unlike a heartbeat.

Then... as suddenly as it had begun... the strands vanished.

The room went still.

Calen let out a breath he didn't know he was holding. "Okay. That was new."

Aelira crouched near the pedestal. Her voice was quiet now, more measured. "It reacted to you first. The glyphs only lit up when you touched the wall. This... whatever this is... it's linked to your bloodline."

"I don't have a bloodline," Calen said, voice flat. "I was found drifting in a pod off the rim colonies. Nobody knows where I came from. Including me."

She looked up at him. "Maybe this place does."

That landed like a stone in his chest.

Behind them, the wall sealed silently, cutting them off from the canyon and the world above. But neither moved. Neither panicked.

There was something sacred here. And something dangerous.

"This isn't a ruin," Calen said. "It's a key."

"To what?" Aelira asked.

He looked at the sphere — the ancient tech humming softly, patient as time itself.

"To everything."

CHAPTER FOUR: THE SPARK BENEATH

The vault's hum deepened.

It started in the walls — a low, resonant tone that vibrated through Calen's chest like the pulse of a giant's heart. The circuitry etched into the panels brightened, their glow shifting from soft blue to a hot, molten gold.

Aelira stepped back from the pedestal. "It's reacting again."

"No," Calen said, his voice hoarse. "It's waking up."

The sphere above the pedestal flared — not light, but memory. A sudden *rush* of images slammed into Calen's mind. He staggered.

—A city of glass and fire, spiralling towers crowned with   flame—
—A voice, deep and ancient: "The Flame must not be broken."
—A hand reaching through smoke—his own?—grasping a small, crying child wrapped in white—
—And a blade, shining with runes, plunged into a seal of stone—

He collapsed to one knee, gasping. The air smelled like ash.

"Calen!" Aelira rushed to his side, kneeling, her hand on his shoulder. "What did you see?"

He blinked, eyes wild. "I... I don't know. A place. A memory that isn't mine. But I felt it. Like I lived it."

The sphere dimmed again, returning to its quiet spin.

Aelira steadied him, her hand still on his arm. "The Starborn Vaults. They were built with memory-mirrors. Fragments of truth encoded in crystal. You triggered it. Not me."

Calen looked up at her. "What does that mean?"

"It means you're not just connected to this," she said quietly. "You're *part* of it."

Before either of them could speak again, a new sound shattered the quiet.

A deep mechanical *crack*.

The pedestal sank into the floor. The walls around them shifted, the panels rippling like liquid stone. One of the conduits above sparked violently. Another burst.

"Time to go!" Calen shouted, already grabbing her arm.

They ran — retracing their steps toward the entrance, but the wall was gone. In its place, a spiralling corridor now stood, lit by pulsing strips of light that ran like veins through the floor.

"It's redirecting us," Aelira said. "The vault is alive."

"Can it tell we're not supposed to be here?" Calen asked.

She glanced at him. "Or that we are."

They raced down the corridor, ducking low-hanging conduits and sidestepping fallen debris. The floor shifted beneath them, grinding as if adjusting to their path. Twice they had to jump cracks opening beneath their feet. Once, Calen grabbed Aelira's hand and didn't let go.

When the final door burst open before them, it led to a narrow fissure — sunlight above, hot, and sharp.

"Boost me," Aelira said, already climbing.

Calen locked his hands and pushed her upward. She caught the edge of the ravine wall and pulled herself out. Then turned, reaching down.

"Your turn."

He grabbed her wrist and hauled himself up beside her just as the vault behind them collapsed inward with a deafening roar. Dust exploded into the sky. The entrance vanished beneath rock and silence.

They lay there, side by side, panting in the golden light.

Neither spoke for a long time.

Then Calen turned his head to her. "So That was intense."

Aelira let out a soft breath — almost a laugh. "You always make jokes after almost dying?"

"It's better than screaming."

She turned her face to him. "You saw something real back there."

"I don't know what it was. But it was waiting for me."

She hesitated. Then said, softer, "I think... I was waiting too."

The moment stretched.

He reached out, brushing a strand of dust-matted white hair from her cheek. She didn't flinch.

She didn't smile, either. But her silver eyes didn't leave his.

Not yet. But soon.

Then she sat up and stood, offering him her hand.

"Come on, Catalyst," she said.

He took it.

CHAPTER FIVE: FIRE IN THE BLOOD

They made camp beneath the jagged arms of an ancient, petrified tree, its twisted limbs reaching into the dusk like frozen claws. The heat of the day had faded, replaced by the crisp hush of Nytharis' nightfall. The triple moons rose over the canyon rim, casting fractured shadows across the sand.

Calen knelt beside a small firepit, coaxing a flame to life with a flick of his wrist-igniter. Sparks flared, and soon a steady orange glow danced between the rocks.

Aelira sat nearby, her back to the fire, watching the stars emerge. She hadn't spoken much since they'd escaped the vault. But her posture had shifted — less guarded now, more... present.

Calen passed her a canteen and a ration pack. "Gourmet desert cuisine. Try not to swoon."

She opened it with a quiet smirk. "Your survival skills are impressive."

"Thanks. They were taught by necessity, not choice."

"Most of the best things are."

They ate in silence for a time, broken only by the occasional crackle of the fire and the wind curling through the canyon. Then Calen leaned back on his elbows, gaze on the moons.

"I wasn't kidding about not knowing who I am."

Aelira didn't turn.

"Pods don't just drift out past the rim," he continued. "Someone sent me away. Someone wanted me gone."

Her voice was soft, but steady. "Or someone wanted to protect you."

He glanced at her.

She still didn't look his way, but her fingers curled tighter around the canteen.

"You don't run without a reason," she said. "Sometimes that reason is fear. Sometimes it's love."

Calen studied her in the firelight. "Is that why you're running?"

She finally turned her head, meeting his eyes. "I'm not running, Rourke. I'm surviving. There's a difference."

"I believe you. But it doesn't mean you're not still carrying it."

Aelira let out a breath — slow, controlled — as if letting go of something she'd been holding for too long.

"The Iron Rebellion murdered my guard, hunted my ship, and shot me down over a dead planet," she said quietly. "I haven't stopped moving since. Every step I take is for Zephyra. For my father. For the blood I carry."

"The blood of kings," Calen murmured.

"No." Her voice was firm. "The blood of my people. My duty isn't about a throne. It's about making sure Zephyra still *exists* for someone to sit on it."

He nodded slowly. "That's a heavy burden."

She looked at him again. "So is not knowing why you matter."

The words struck deep.

They sat quietly after that, the fire crackling between them, shadows dancing on the canyon walls. The silence wasn't awkward — it felt like something sacred, something earned.

After a while, Aelira reached into her satchel and pulled out a small metallic shard — curved, etched with a symbol that looked like fire flowing into wings.

"This was my mother's," she said. "She died when I was young. I keep it close when things feel... uncertain."

Calen reached into his coat and pulled out a fragment of crystal — dull grey, barely larger than a coin.

"I've had this since I was found. No markings. No clue where it came from. But every time I think about tossing it... I can't."

They stared at each other for a long moment.

Then, without a word, she leaned closer and held her shard near his crystal.

For a heartbeat, nothing happened.

Then both pieces shimmered — faintly — and pulsed with the same rhythm.

Calen inhaled sharply.

"Looks like they remember each other," Aelira said softly.

He didn't answer.

Instead, he watched her in the firelight — white hair glowing like silver flame, eyes reflecting not just light, but something deeper.

"Why did you trust me?" he asked.

Aelira tilted her head. "I didn't."

"Thanks."

"I *chose* to trust you. There's a difference."

That made him laugh — low and real. "You always split hairs like that?"

"Only when the truth matters."

She turned back toward the stars. But this time, she sat a little closer. And Calen didn't move away.

The fire crackled between them.

But it wasn't the only thing burning.

CHAPTER SIX: THE ENEMY ABOVE

The crackle of the fire had dwindled to embers, the heat now gentle, the silence thick.

Then Calen sat bolt upright.

A low rumble trembled through the ground — not seismic. Not natural.

Aelira was already on her feet, eyes scanning the sky. "That's not thunder."

He followed her gaze — up past the canyon rim, where one of the triple moons was now half-obscured by a shadow far too angular to be natural.

A ship.

Sleek, black, dagger-shaped — flying without running lights. Silent as death. A scout-class interceptor, Iron Rebellion standard.

Calen swore. "We have minutes. Maybe less."

Aelira grabbed her satchel. "We can't outrun it on foot."

"We don't need to," he said, snapping open his scope. "We just need to *disappear*."

He dashed to a cluster of rocks nearby, where his cloaking field projector was hidden beneath a tarp. It wasn't built for stealth under direct scan — but with enough interference, enough misdirection...

"I need ten seconds," he said.

The ship turned, angling toward them.

"You have five," Aelira said, drawing her blade — its edge already glowing with latent energy.

Calen's fingers flew over the controls, rerouting power from the scanner to the emitter.

The sky lit up.

A bright red beam lanced down from the ship's undercarriage — sweeping the ground like a searchlight. Dust exploded in columns as it cut across the canyon.

Then it *stopped* — right on their camp.

"Too late!" Calen shouted.

The air ignited.

He tackled Aelira just as the beam hit the camp. Their firepit vaporized. Their gear turned molten. The petrified tree shattered into dust.

The blast wave threw them both down the slope.

Calen landed hard on his side. Aelira hit shoulder-first and rolled, coming up with a wince, blade still in hand.

The scout ship descended with terrifying grace — repulsors whispering rather than roaring, silent as falling ash.

Then the hatch opened.

Three figures leapt out — tall, armoured in black plating etched with crimson sigils. Their helmets resembled skulls, segmented and smooth, with no visible eye-sockets — only a vertical slit glowing with red light.

Aelira rose first. "Reapers."

Calen spat blood and stood. "What kind of name is—"

The first one raised a gauntlet. It hissed — then fired.

A plasma bolt scorched the space where Calen had been a moment before.

He dove, rolled, came up with his rifle. "Guess we're doing this the hard way."

The fight exploded.

Aelira was already moving — a blur of white and blue, her blade arcing through the dark like lightning. Calen covered her with precision shots, keeping the Reapers staggered and off balance.

One of them turned and barked something into its comms — and Calen heard it.

A name.

A name he hadn't used since he was a child. A name he couldn't even remember until now.

"—*Catalyst Prime*—"

He froze. Just for a moment.

That moment almost got him killed.

The Reaper lunged — blade out.

But Aelira was faster.

She slammed into the Reaper, knocking it off balance, her own blade cleaving through its Armour. Sparks exploded. The thing twitched — then collapsed in a heap.

"Stay with me!" she shouted.

Calen shook off the shock. "They knew my name."

She didn't answer — because the last Reaper had drawn something from its belt.

A small, glowing orb.

"No—!" Aelira shouted.

It hit the ground between them.

A pulse wave *slammed* outward — bright, violet, silent.

Calen felt his muscles lock. His thoughts scatter.

Then — *darkness.*

CHAPTER SEVEN: AWAKENING

The fire crackled low, casting flickering shadows against the canyon walls. The hidden shelter Calen had chosen was little more than a narrow cleft in the rock, camouflaged by centuries of windblown ash and twisted roots. But it was safe — for now.

Aelira sat cross-legged near the fire, her blade across her knees. Calen could see the pain she tried to mask. Her side still bled beneath the field dressing, and her posture was tense, alert, even in exhaustion.

He dropped a ration pack beside her. "Not much, but it's warm."

She nodded in thanks, peeling back the wrapper. The silence stretched between them—not awkward but weighted. Calen sat opposite her, arms resting on his knees, watching the fire more than her. But his mind was nowhere near the flames.

"What you said earlier," he began, voice low, "Zephyra. That place. I've seen it."

She looked up, eyes narrowing. "In visions?"

"Dreams. For over a year now. Always the same. Twin suns. A canyon. And you."

She didn't answer. Instead, she reached into a pouch at her belt and pulled out a small crystal shard, glowing faintly violet. It pulsed when she held it toward him.

He leaned forward. "What is that?"

"A memory crystal," she said. "Attuned to Starborn signatures."

"I'm not Starborn."

"Then it shouldn't do this."

The crystal's glow intensified.

Calen stared at it. "What does it mean?"

"It means," Aelira said softly, "you're more than what you've been told."

He felt his pulse spike. "I don't even know who I *am*, Aelira. I don't remember anything before my sixteenth year. Just woke up in a Concord med-facility with scars and nightmares."

"Someone hid you. Changed your records. Buried your origin." She looked at him, her expression unreadable. "But something remained. In your dreams. Your instincts."

A distant howl echoed through the canyon. Calen stood quickly, scanning the cliffs.

"Relax," she said. "The wards I cast will hold for tonight."

He sat again, but his body stayed coiled.

"You said 'Starborn'," he said finally. "Like it means something more than myth."

Aelira's eyes reflected the firelight. "It's not a myth. The Starborn were real — are real. Rare, scattered. Children of starlight, born in cycles. You feel it, don't you? The pull?"

He hesitated... then nodded. "Like something's always burning behind the veil. Waiting."

"That's your birthright."

Suddenly, the fire flared.

No wood shifted. No wind blew. But the flames turned *blue*, rising two meters high in a blink.

Calen leapt up, heart pounding. "What the hell?"

Aelira stared at him. "That was *you*."

He backed away from the fire, breath ragged. "No. I didn't—"

"You're awakening, Calen. The vault... the battle... your proximity to me. It's catalysing it."

Blue sparks leapt from his hands and vanished into the air.

"No," he whispered. "This isn't me."

But somewhere, deep inside, it *was*.

And far above them, the Iron Rebellion's command ship intercepted a surge of unfamiliar energy—pure, radiant, unmistakable.

One word whispered through the rebel channel.

"Starborn."

CHAPTER EIGHT: ECHOES AND FLAME

The ravine was silent as twilight deepened, shadows creeping like long fingers along the jagged rock walls. Calen and Aelira sat by a narrow fire, flames low, cautious. The heat from the day still lingered in the rocks, radiating warmth into the cooling air. Above them, stars began to prick through the purple dusk, slowly unveiling the great celestial dome.

Aelira's white hair caught the firelight like a halo. She sat cross-legged, wrapping a strip of cloth around her ribs, wincing slightly as she tightened it. Calen offered her a pain-stem patch from his med-kit, but she waved him off with a slight smirk.

"You're persistent," she said.

"Better than being dead," he replied, his voice quiet.

He caught her watching him again—not just with curiosity, but caution. Or maybe it was calculation.

"You don't trust me," he said.

"I don't trust anyone," she answered. "But you haven't tried to kill me. That's worth something."

"Glad to be of service." He paused, then added, "You said something earlier—Zephyra. That's where you're from?"

"Yes. Or was. Before the rebellion turned my home into a battlefield." Her voice went quiet. "Before they murdered my father."

The fire popped softly. Calen looked into the flames, unsure what to say.

"I keep dreaming about that name," he finally said. "Zephyra. Long before I came here. And... you."

Her gaze sharpened. "Me?"

"In the dream, you're standing in the wind. Silver eyes. No face, not at first, but... it was always you."

Aelira didn't speak for a moment. Then she said, "The Starborn always dream."

Calen turned his head. "What?"

She rose slowly to her feet and crossed to him, her voice low. "You don't know what you are, do you?"

He stood too, tension crackling in the air.

"I'm just a scavenger."

"No," she said gently. "You're something much more."

He didn't understand. Before he could press her, a pulse of pain surged behind his eyes. The world spun. Aelira shouted his name as he staggered back.

And then the dream returned.

Flashes. A temple bathed in starlight. A voice not his own. *Awaken, Catalyst.*

He hit the ground hard, gasping.

Calen woke to Aelira crouched beside him; her hand pressed to his forehead.

"You passed out," she said.

"Thanks for the news flash," he groaned, blinking at the starlit sky.

"There was a flare of energy," she murmured. "Like a Starborn awakening."

"You keep using that word."

"Because you *are* one."

He sat up slowly, rubbing his temples. "I need answers."

She didn't respond—but instead turned toward the mouth of the ravine. "You'll have them soon. Come look."

Calen followed her gaze. A soft blue glow pulsed on the horizon. Concord emergency beacon.

"It's only ten klicks," she said. "But that signal's fresh. Someone made it to the surface."

He nodded. "Then let's find them before the Iron Rebellion does."

The trek took half the day. The beacon led them into a narrow canyon strewn with jagged stones and strange, fossilized structures. Aelira moved like she knew the place—or at least understood its dangers.

They reached the source. The beacon pulsed from the centre of an overgrown ruin—a circular platform marked with ancient glyphs and shattered obelisks. A dead pilot lay slumped nearby, uniform scorched.

"No survivors," Calen muttered, scanning the wreckage. "This wasn't a crash. This was execution."

Aelira knelt beside a stone column, brushing dust away to reveal the emblem of a phoenix surrounded by seven stars.

"The Temple of Echoes," she whispered. "One of the ancient vaults of the Starborn."

"Vaults?"

"Places of memory. Of awakening." She stepped forward and placed her hand on the stone.

The platform responded. A low vibration hummed beneath their feet, and a ring of symbols lit up.

Calen tensed. "You activated it."

"No," she said. "*You* did."

The light flared—and above them, high in the cloud-choked sky, a satellite turned its eye.

The Iron Rebellion had found them.

CHAPTER NINE: THE DEPTHS BELOW

The circular platform hummed beneath their feet as the glyphs around its edge glowed with a deep azure light. Calen glanced at Aelira, but her attention was locked on the Centre of the structure. A ring of ancient runes pulsed in sequence—inviting, almost sentient.

With a deep, grinding sound, the Centre of the dais split apart and began to descend. A narrow spiral staircase unfurled from the stone like coiled ribbon, plunging into the darkness below.

"I guess that's our welcome mat," Calen said, aiming his torch into the gloom.

Aelira nodded solemnly. "This place responds to Starborn blood. It was built for your kind."

"Our kind," he corrected.

She gave him a small, unreadable smile and descended the steps.

As they moved deeper underground, the temperature dropped. The air thickened, laced with the scent of ozone and something older dust, maybe. Or time itself. The walls were carved with intricate reliefs: celestial bodies, radiant figures, and a blazing star at the Centre of every scene.

Calen ran his fingers over one panel that showed a man standing alone before a crowd, flame spilling from his hands. "These people… they worshipped the Starborn?"

"Some did. Others feared them. The Starborn were not just warriors, but keepers of balance. Catalysts."

"There's that word again."

Aelira stopped before a vast stone door etched with twin spirals. She pressed her hand to the Centre.

"I believe you're the last Catalyst, Calen. And the universe has been waiting for you to wake up."

The door groaned open.

They stepped into a massive chamber lit by a hovering ring of energy. The walls were layered with crystalline conduits, some pulsing faintly. A central plinth rose from the floor, surrounded by seven glowing orbs—each showing a different world.

"This is a Vault of Memory," Aelira said reverently. "Echoes of what came before are stored here."

Calen approached one of the orbs. As his hand neared, the image shimmered—and he was pulled into a vision.

He stood on a battlefield beneath a storm-wracked sky. A woman with wings of fire soared above him, shouting commands. Beside him, warriors made of light clashed with shadows that hissed and writhed.

Calen raised his hand—and flame surged forth, consuming the dark.

A voice echoed through the scene: *He is the Flame. The Catalyst. The one who breaks the cycle.*

Then, silence.

He gasped, staggering back. The orb dimmed.

"You saw something," Aelira said.

"A memory. A war. Me—fighting. Using... fire."

She looked at him with something between fear and awe. "Then the Vault has accepted you."

Before he could respond, the chamber shuddered. A deep rumble echoed from the corridor.

"Not good," Calen muttered.

Stone cracked—and from the shadows emerged a construct of obsidian and bone. Towering, spider-like, its limbs etched with glowing crimson. A guardian.

Aelira raised her blade. "These vaults were not left undefended."

Calen's hand burned—the same fire from the vision tingled beneath his skin.

He stepped forward.

"Then let's see what I can do."

CHAPTER TEN: THE CATALYST'S FIRE

The guardian lunged forward, its bladed limbs striking the stone floor with thunderous cracks. Calen dove aside just as one talon cleaved through the spot he'd been standing, sending shards of rock flying. The obsidian creature turned with eerie grace; its glowing crimson eyes fixed on him.

Aelira darted in, her blade flashing, slicing a shallow groove along one of its legs. Sparks flew, but the guardian barely reacted. She ducked under a sweeping claw and rolled, landing in a crouch beside Calen.

"It's heavily shielded!" she shouted, catching her breath.

"No kidding!" Calen replied, pressing his back against a pillar. His heart thundered, blood rushing in his ears. His right hand still burned—alive with the lingering energy from the Vault's memory. It wasn't just warmth. It was *power*—raw, ancient, waiting to be wielded.

He closed his eyes and focused, reaching into the sensation. It felt like a firestorm behind his ribs, chaotic and primal. A roaring presence that had always been there, waiting.

The memory returned—the woman with wings, the battlefield, the flame spilling from his hands.

You are the Catalyst.

The truth wasn't whispered. It boomed like a drumbeat in his soul.

He stepped out from cover.

The guardian shrieked and charged.

Calen raised his hand.

The fire came.

A jet of flame spiralled from his palm, blazing through the air and slamming into the construct's chest. The force staggered the guardian, pushing it back as flames licked across its obsidian shell, seeking cracks in its runes.

"Calen!" Aelira called, stunned. "You—how?"

"I don't know!" he gasped. "But I *feel* it—it's like breathing fire and lightning!"

The guardian recovered quickly, rushing him with jagged limbs extended. Calen ducked under a strike, then lashed out with a sweep of fire that curved like a whip. The heat scorched the stone floor, gouging glowing trenches in its wake.

Aelira leapt in from the other side, using his distraction to plunge her blade into the guardian's exposed joint. This time, the metal hissed and cracked. The creature recoiled with an unearthly screech.

"You're weakening it!" she cried. "Keep going!"

Calen nodded, sweat streaming down his face. He forced himself to focus again—not just on destruction, but *direction*. The fire bent to his will, moving like a living thing.

He stepped into the centre of the chamber, hands raised. The construct reared, sensing the shift.

Calen clenched his fists.

The flames erupted in twin arcs—searing ribbons of power that carved into the guardian's chest and core. Its runes flared once, then fractured. With a deafening boom, the creature collapsed in on itself. Its limbs folded. Its core went dark.

The chamber fell silent.

Smoke curled upward from molten cracks in the floor. The stench of scorched stone and ozone lingered. Calen stood panting, fire flickering faintly across his knuckles. His entire body trembled.

Aelira approached cautiously, lowering her sword. She reached out and touched his hand, her fingers brushing against his skin. "You just awakened," she said softly. "The Vault didn't just recognize you—it *unlocked* you."

Calen met her eyes, disoriented. "It's... overwhelming. Like there's a storm inside me. I barely held it together."

"But you did."

She guided him gently to a nearby step. They sat side by side in the lingering glow of the fading runes. Her voice dropped. "When I was young, I heard stories of the Catalyst. The one who wouldn't just fight darkness—but *change* the course of fate. I used to think it was myth."

"You think it's me?"

"I *know* it is."

Calen looked down at his hands, the memory of flame still burning in his veins. "Then I hope I'm ready."

Aelira hesitated, then reached out and brushed a strand of ash from his cheek. Her touch lingered.

"You're not alone, Calen."

Their eyes held. For a moment, the silence between them was charged not with danger—but something deeper, warmer. She leaned closer—then a distant tremor echoed from above.

They both stood in an instant.

"What was that?" Calen asked.

Aelira's expression darkened. "Iron Rebellion dropships. They must've tracked the Vault's activation. We don't have much time."

They turned toward the far corridor, where ancient light pulsed like a heartbeat.

Behind them, the shattered remains of the guardian smouldered—but the fire now burned in Calen's soul.

CHAPTER ELEVEN: THE BROKEN SKY

The ascent from the Vault was steep and narrow, the worn stone steps slick with condensation. Faint vibrations trembled through the ground beneath them—a distant, rhythmic hum that made the ancient walls groan like a living beast.

"They're coming fast," Aelira said, hand gripping the railing as they climbed. Her voice was tight with urgency. "Dropships. At least three."

Calen paused halfway up the steps, glancing toward the light above. The air was tinged with ozone and smoke, and the metallic scent of the guardian's remains still clung to him. "If they followed the energy spike—"

"They'll want what's inside you," she finished grimly. "The fire. The Vault's secrets. They'll rip it out of you if they can."

He exhaled, pulse still thundering from the battle below. The power hadn't faded completely—it still shimmered just beneath his skin like embers waiting for wind.

When they reached the surface, Nytharis greeted them with an angry sky. A thick plume of smoke rose from the northern horizon. The soft red light of the twin suns was gone, replaced by the dull gleam of descending craft.

Dropships. Iron Rebellion.

Calen squinted. "They're landing in the canyon."

Aelira brought up her wrist console and tapped in a quick scan. A blue projection shimmered into view—three ships, two squadrons of drones, and one human signal among them.

"That signature..." she muttered. "Commander Varik. He's one of their top hunters. We're not facing a search team. This is a *recovery* operation."

"Meaning?"

"Meaning they think the Catalyst is active. And they're here to bring you in—or burn you out."

A low whine echoed through the valley as gunships screamed overhead. A moment later, two scout drones zipped into view, scanning the canyon floor. One veered toward them.

Calen raised his hand instinctively.

"No!" Aelira grabbed his wrist. "If you use your power again so soon—"

The drone fired.

She shoved him behind a boulder, the blast grazing her shoulder. She winced, teeth clenched. Calen rose, fists burning.

"No choice now," he growled.

This time, he didn't summon a firestorm. Just a tight, focused blast—more a lance than a flare. The flame seared through the air and struck the drone cleanly, melting it mid-flight.

The second drone swerved and retreated.

Calen ran to Aelira, who was cradling her arm. "You okay?"

"I'll live." She looked up at him, pain flashing behind her eyes—but also pride. "Your control is improving."

He nodded. "Feels... more natural now. Like the fire knows me."

She smiled faintly. "That's how it starts."

A distant *boom* rumbled the earth—one of the dropships landing hard.

They had minutes at most.

"We need to vanish," Aelira said. "There's a hidden tunnel behind that ridge. If we make it there, we can lose them in the ravines and circle back to the Concord point."

Calen steadied her as they moved quickly across the rocks. The wind had picked up, carrying dust and static. High above, the sky split with lightning that had no storm—just crackling energy bleeding from the edges of the Rebellion's tech.

As they ran, Calen glanced back once.

The canyon behind them was crawling with metal. Drones like locusts, soldiers in dark armour, ships lowering like vultures.

Aelira was right.

They weren't searching.

They were hunting.

And this time, they'd found what they were looking for.

CHAPTER TWELVE: ASH AND ECHOES

The hidden tunnel was carved from ancient basalt, narrow and slick with time. Aelira led the way with a palm light, casting shifting shadows along the soot-streaked walls. Each step echoed like whispers—soft, scattered, uncertain.

Calen followed in silence, keeping one hand close to the wall. His other hand still tingled faintly, the last embers of his fire curled deep in his blood. He couldn't tell if the warmth was comforting or terrifying.

"How far does this go?" he asked quietly.

"About half a kilometre," Aelira replied, glancing back. "It was built by the First Concord, long before the Rebellion. These tunnels were used to transport memory shards—records of the old world."

Calen's brows furrowed. "You mean like data archives?"

"Not just data," she said. "Memories. Echoes of lived experiences. They could be played back with the right crystal interface. That's why they called this place the Temple of Echoes."

They walked on.

Soon, they reached a chamber cut wider than the rest of the tunnel. In the centre stood a small obelisk covered in glowing runes. Aelira knelt beside it and touched the top.

The air changed.

A sudden stillness fell, followed by a ripple of energy that passed through Calen like a wave. And then—

Voices.

A soft chorus of overlapping whispers swirled around them. Not loud. Not clear. But unmistakably human.

Aelira looked up at him. "The obelisk remembers."

Calen stepped closer, his breath hitching as images flickered in the air—phantoms of another time. A man in armour, falling. A woman screaming into fire. A child holding a glowing shard.

"What is this?" he breathed.

"The last days of the Starborn War," Aelira said. "Memories stored by those who died protecting the Catalyst."

One image lingered longer than the rest—a young man, dark-haired and defiant, standing in front of a scorched gate. His eyes were bright with power, and something about him—his stance, his face—felt familiar.

Calen took a step forward, and the figure seemed to look directly at him.

The vision cracked.

The obelisk flared, and a sudden pulse of force shoved them both backward.

Aelira coughed. "It's reacting to you. That's never happened before."

Calen helped her to her feet. "Who was that?"

She hesitated. "One of the original Catalysts. The first to bear the fire. Some say his blood still flows through the chosen line."

Calen swallowed. "You think that's me?"

"I think... the fire chose you. That has to mean something."

A rumble shook the tunnel, deeper than any quake.

Aelira's hand darted to her console. "Rebellion breach. They're trying to collapse the entrance."

Calen looked back toward the long corridor. "How many exits?"

"Just one."

"Then we go forward."

Aelira nodded, already moving. "There's a Concord outpost near the crater rim. If we reach it—"

"We send a warning," Calen said, finishing her thought.

They ran.

Behind them, the whispers faded into the stone.

But Calen knew what he saw wasn't just memory.

It was a message.

And it was meant for him.

CHAPTER THIRTEEN: FIRE UPON THE CRATER

The exit tunnel opened onto a jagged overlook near the crater rim, where the valley floor dropped into a molten sea of red rock and steam. The air was thinner here, laced with ash and ozone, and every breath tasted of scorched iron.

Calen steadied Aelira as they emerged, her wounded shoulder wrapped in a makeshift sling. She hadn't complained once, but the tension in her jaw told him everything he needed to know.

He scanned the skyline. "No sign of Rebellion troops—yet."

"They'll be on us within minutes," Aelira said, voice low. "The blast didn't slow them for long."

A burst of static came from her wrist console. She tapped it. A faint voice crackled through.

"Concord outpost Aegis-9, this is Field Agent Aelira Vaelori. We have the Catalyst. Immediate evac request at crater coordinates Delta-Zero. Repeat, evac request—"

A pause. Then: "Copy that, Agent Vaelori. ETA, six minutes. Hold your position."

"Six minutes is an eternity," Calen muttered.

She glanced at him. "Then let's make it count."

Movement below—dark shapes slithering from the trees near the crater's far edge. Drones, quick and silent. Behind them, Rebellion soldiers in adaptive armour advanced in a pincer movement.

Calen's heartbeat thundered. "Too many to hold."

Aelira unslung her sidearm. "We don't hold. We delay."

But Calen stepped forward, fire already threading through his veins.

"No," he said. "We *rise*."

He closed his eyes, drawing the heat from the stone beneath his boots. The crater itself responded—like something ancient remembered him. Sparks leapt from his fingertips. His breath came slower now. Controlled.

He raised his arms.

The fire obeyed.

Flames erupted in a circle before the advancing line, driving back the first wave. Drones exploded in the blast. Calen's stance was firm, his aura blazing like a sun reborn. His eyes glowed faintly.

He was no longer *becoming* the Catalyst.

He *was* the Catalyst.

Gunfire lit the edges of the crater. Aelira fired methodically, covering his flank. The world tilted into chaos—but within it, Calen stood as the eye of the storm.

Then a shadow moved through the fire.

A figure clad in obsidian armour strode into view, flames licking off without harm. Tall. Broad. Radiating malice.

"Commander Varik," Aelira said under her breath.

Varik stopped, assessing them. "So it's true. The Catalyst lives again."

Calen raised his chin. "You're not taking me."

Varik smirked. "No. I'm *breaking* you."

He raised a gauntleted fist—and the fire obeyed him, parting like a curtain. A wave of concussive force blasted toward Calen, knocking him off his feet.

"Calen!" Aelira cried, lunging forward.

But Calen was already rising, blood on his lip, fury in his heart. He gritted his teeth and flung his hand forward—flames bending, coiling, lashing like serpents.

Varik caught the blast with one armoured palm—but even he staggered.

The sky rumbled.

Above, a streak of silver descended—a Concord dropship, sleek and fast, roaring toward them.

Varik turned, calculating.

Aelira didn't wait. She grabbed Calen's wrist and sprinted for the ledge.

"They're landing on the lower shelf!" she shouted.

Gunfire chased them, but Calen spun, fire trailing behind like a burning wall, shielding their retreat.

The dropship's hatch opened. A voice barked: "Go! Go!"

They leapt.

Strong arms caught them, hauling them inside. The hatch sealed. The ship lurched into the sky.

Calen collapsed against the hull, chest heaving. Aelira slid down beside him, her face pale, lips tight with pain—but her eyes never left his.

"You're not just a weapon," she whispered.

He met her gaze. "Then what am I?"

She reached out and touched his hand.

"Something new."

Below, the crater burned.

CHAPTER FOURTEEN: FLIGHT AND FLAME

The dropship roared skyward, engines screaming against the thin atmosphere as the chaos of the crater shrank behind them. Flames still licked the rim, and smoke coiled into the sky like the breath of some buried titan.

Inside, everything rattled. Aelira gripped a metal brace with one hand, the other pressed tightly to her wounded shoulder. Blood seeped through the wrappings, dark and slow. Across from her, Calen sat with his back against the hull, legs sprawled, chest still heaving with the remnants of fire and fear.

Neither spoke for a moment.

The cabin lights flickered. A medic in Concord grey dropped beside Aelira, already prepping a stim injector. "You'll be fine," he said. "Shrapnel missed the artery. You're lucky."

"Not luck," she murmured. "Just timing."

Calen leaned his head back, eyes closed. He still felt the fire simmering beneath his skin—quiet now, but not gone. Like it waited. Like it *watched*.

"You okay?" Aelira's voice was soft but edged with tension.

He opened his eyes. "I don't know what that was back there. I wasn't just using the fire. It felt like…it was using *me*."

Aelira nodded slowly. "That's the cost. The Catalyst power isn't something you command. It bonds. It learns you."

"That's not comforting."

"It's not meant to be."

The ship rocked as it passed into a higher stratum. Through the narrow viewport, Nytharis spread out below—scarred, smouldering, beautiful in a harsh way. Calen watched the crater disappear in the distance.

Aelira spoke again, more quietly. "Varik shouldn't have been able to part your fire. That was…impossible."

"He did."

She nodded. "Which means he's no ordinary commander. And he's coming for us."

The medic moved to Calen, checking vitals. "His temperature's elevated," he muttered. "Still burning something off."

"Let him," Aelira said. "He needs to learn what balance feels like."

Calen's voice was hoarse. "I need to learn *what I am*."

A silence passed between them.

Then Aelira reached into a side pouch on her belt and pulled out a worn data shard. "This belonged to my brother. He was the last known Catalyst before you. He died trying to resist the Rebellion's first wave."

Calen looked at the shard, hesitating.

"I want you to see what he saw," she said. "Maybe it'll help you understand what's coming. And who you'll have to become."

He took it slowly, as if it might burn him.

The dropship's pilot chimed in over the comms. "Approaching Concord Station Vestra. ETA, two minutes. Prep for descent."

Calen gripped the shard tighter. "Two minutes," he whispered. "That's all it takes to change everything."

Aelira leaned toward him, her voice low. "Then make it count."

CHAPTER FIFTEEN: VESTRA STATION

The dropship landed with a metallic hiss, settling into the cradle of Vestra Station's docking platform. Hydraulic arms clamped down, locking the vessel in place, while the hangar lights bathed everything in sterile white.

As the ramp descended, Calen followed Aelira into the cool interior of the station, limping slightly from a muscle strain he hadn't noticed until now. The contrast from the burnt wilds outside was jarring— smooth corridors, humming walls, the smell of recycled air and disinfectant.

Concord soldiers in polished grey armour snapped to attention as they passed. Some glanced at Aelira with recognition; fewer still looked to Calen with a mix of curiosity and subtle awe. News travelled fast, apparently.

A woman stood waiting at the end of the corridor— older, with silver-streaked hair pulled into a tight braid and a datapad in her hand. Her eyes, though tired, burned sharp.

"Commander Vaelori," she greeted. "You're late."

Aelira gave the faintest nod. "Blame the Iron Rebellion. They crashed the party."

The woman's gaze turned to Calen. "So this is him."

Calen straightened instinctively.

"He's the one," Aelira said. "And he needs answers."

The woman extended a hand. "Director Selene, Vestra Station Intelligence."

Calen shook it. Her grip was firm.

"I've arranged secure quarters for you both," she said. "And there's a briefing chamber ready whenever you're stable. But first—medical scan. Protocol."

They were led to a sleek room where med-techs ran scans, collected samples, and muttered in low tones. Calen's internal temperature still ran high, but his vitals had stabilized. The fire wasn't burning him from the inside anymore—but it *was* still there.

Once cleared, they were taken to a quiet room overlooking the stars. Vestra's orbital position allowed for a breathtaking view of Nytharis' shattered surface below.

"I hate being inside," Calen muttered.

Aelira raised a brow. "You prefer dirt and craters?"

"At least you know what's coming at you out there."

She didn't disagree.

Selene returned, this time with a holoprojector in hand. She placed it on the table and activated it. A shimmering display of ancient runes and a planetary schematic flickered to life.

"This," she said, "is what your brother died protecting. A location buried beneath the southern pole—sealed for centuries. We believe it's the origin point of the Catalyst line."

Calen leaned in. "Why hasn't it been opened?"

"Because no one alive had the fire to do it," Selene said. "Until now."

Aelira turned to him, her voice soft. "This is where your journey leads next."

Outside the viewport, lightning cracked through a distant storm system on the planet below.

Calen's eyes didn't leave the map. "Then we'd better get moving."

CHAPTER SIXTEEN: THE SOUTHERN SEAL

The journey south was quiet.

Calen stood at the edge of the viewing deck aboard the orbital shuttle, watching Nytharis spin slowly beneath them. Storms brewed over the equator, glowing faintly with flashes of green lightning. The surface below looked cracked and ancient, like the fossilized skin of something long dead.

He hadn't said much since leaving Vestra Station. His mind churned like the storm belts below, wrapped around visions he couldn't fully grasp. Every instinct in him said this was important. More than that—*inevitable*.

Beside him, Aelira didn't speak for some time.

"You don't have to go alone," she said finally.

"I'm not," he replied. "You're coming with me."

Her lips twitched. "I meant in your head. You've been distant since the station."

"I saw the recordings from your brother," Calen murmured. "He was stronger than I'll ever be. And he still died."

"He died trying to protect something worth more than himself," she said. "That's strength. And you've got it."

The shuttle descended into the upper atmosphere, buffeted by violent winds. Selene had warned them the southern pole was unstable riddled with fractures, magnetic anomalies, and tectonic quakes. It was a wasteland that swallowed satellites whole. No one came here unless they had a death wish—or a destiny.

But buried beneath all of it was the Seal. A structure older than any known Concord record. And possibly the birthplace of the Catalyst force.

As they neared the coordinates, the landscape shifted ridges of black glass, twisted rock, and shimmering frost. The sun barely reached here. The temperature plunged. The sky above had a thin, torn quality—as if the planet itself were holding its breath.

The shuttle touched down with a hiss, stabilizers groaning against the uneven terrain. The hull creaked. Outside, static lightning rippled across the surface.

Calen stepped out first.

The cold hit him like a hammer.

Breath misted instantly. Even through the reinforced suit, he felt it bite—sharp and bone-deep. The air tasted metallic, thin and strange. His boots crunched over crystalline dust that shimmered faintly beneath his steps.

Aelira followed, activating a pulse beacon. "The entrance should be sixty meters northwest."

They moved cautiously, climbing over slick ridges and jagged spires. The silence here was complete—not even wind, only the hum of the pulse beacon and the soft hiss of their breath.

Then they saw it: a spiral staircase descending into a crevice hidden between broken rocks. The steps were carved—not naturally formed. And etched into every riser were glowing lines of red and gold.

Catalyst script.

Calen reached out, brushing his fingers across a symbol. It flared warm beneath his touch.

"I can feel it," he said. "Calling."

"Then answer it."

They descended.

Each step vibrated faintly, as though reacting to his presence. At the bottom, a great obsidian door stood sealed by overlapping rings—each humming with faint energy. The entire chamber pulsed with a dormant heartbeat.

Aelira scanned the surface, but her tech pinged negative. "No Concord signature. Nothing I can override."

Calen stepped forward. "But I can."

He placed both hands on the centre ring.

A surge of heat pulsed outward, and the rings began to spin, glowing brighter. His vision blurred. For a heartbeat, he wasn't on Nytharis anymore—he was standing in a burning void, surrounded by whispers in forgotten tongues. Shapes loomed around him—figures of flame and shadow, indistinct but watching.

A voice echoed: *"Only flame awakens what flame has hidden."*

Then the door shuddered.

With a thunderous groan, it opened inward.

Beyond lay a corridor, lined with crystal veins and metallic roots that pulsed faintly with life.

Aelira's voice was reverent. "We just crossed into something sacred."

Calen stared ahead. "Or something buried for a reason."

They stepped inside, the door closing behind them, sealing the Southern Seal from the world once more.

CHAPTER SEVENTEEN: HEART OF THE HOLLOW

The corridor sloped downward, curving in a slow spiral lit by flickering veins of crystal embedded in the walls. A low hum thrummed beneath their feet—subsonic, constant, and unnerving. Calen felt it in his bones.

He walked at the front, one hand brushing the smooth metal wall. The surface pulsed faintly, as if sensing him. Every few steps, symbols ignited along the metal—Catalyst script responding to something in his presence.

Aelira followed close behind, her steps careful, eyes narrowed. "This place shouldn't exist. Not like this. This is beyond pre-Concord."

"It's alive," Calen said.

They passed beneath a massive arch of obsidian and gold. Beyond it, the spiral opened into a wide chamber. The air changed—denser, charged. The walls were carved with flowing script, interwoven with pictographs: stars falling, fire blooming from hands, eyes watching from darkness.

At the chamber's centre stood a pedestal of stone and metal, its top shaped like an open palm. Calen approached, drawn to it by something more than curiosity. His skin prickled.

"Are you sure?" Aelira asked. Her voice was tense, cautious.

"No," he said. "But I have to."

He stepped forward.

The moment his hand touched the pedestal, the chamber reacted. Light burst through the walls—streams of golden-red energy tracing through ancient grooves. The floor trembled beneath them, a deep vibration that resonated in his chest.

Calen's vision whited out.

He stood in a field of ash beneath a black sky. Great spires loomed in the distance, burning from within. The air crackled with static. Around him, figures moved—robed, tall, indistinct. Their eyes glowed like twin stars, flickering like flames in a storm.

One stepped forward. "Starborn," the figure said. Its voice echoed like it came from a well of time, distant and layered.

Calen tried to speak but found he had no mouth. Only thought. *What is this?*

The figure extended a hand and pressed it to his chest. The moment of contact ignited a rush of images: a child suspended in a glass pod; a woman screaming behind a sealed door; a great mountain splitting open in fire. He felt the heat, the terror, the loneliness.

"You were made to remember," the voice whispered. "You carry more than blood. You carry legacy. Catalyst. Choice."

Then the vision shifted—brief flashes of war, of stars going dark, of two lovers reaching for each other across a broken battlefield. A great machine, half-buried in a desert. The sound of a heartbeat. His own?

Then it all shattered.

He fell backward, gasping, the weight of it all slamming into his chest. The chamber reformed around him, cold and quiet.

Aelira was gripping his arm. "Calen! You dropped like a stone. You stopped breathing."

He blinked up at her. His hand tingled where it had touched the pedestal. "I saw... something. A memory? A warning. A past that doesn't belong to me, but... it's inside me."

She helped him sit up. Her voice, still shaken, softened. "The Catalyst doesn't just store power. It stores *truth*. And it shares that truth with those who bear the mark."

Calen looked toward the walls, where the glowing script had faded into silence. The air still felt charged, like something had only just left. "There's something buried here. A power... maybe even a warning."

Aelira glanced once more at the pedestal, then back to him. "Let's find out which."

They turned together, deeper into the hollow.

Behind them, the pedestal's light pulsed once more.

A heartbeat.

CHAPTER EIGHTEEN: EMBERS OF THE PAST

The corridor narrowed the farther they walked, forcing Aelira and Calen to move single file. The air was growing colder now, laced with the faint scent of ozone and something metallic. Their footsteps echoed, too loud in the stillness, as if the ancient place resented the intrusion. Ahead, dim shapes began to form—arched frames of ancient metal struts and glass that caught and held the faint light from their path like the bones of something long-dead.

"What is this place?" Aelira murmured, drawing her coat tighter.

"Looks like a control chamber," Calen said. "But way older than anything we've seen."

They stepped into a vast dome-like room. The floor was etched with circular patterns—interlocking rings carved so precisely they looked like they might spin at any moment. Around the perimeter stood thick pylons, each about three meters tall, their tops fused with dormant crystal orbs.

Aelira crouched, brushing dust from one of the rings. "Starforged alloy. These markings... they're not just decorative. They're conduits."

Calen nodded slowly, eyes scanning the chamber. "It's a memory core."

He approached one of the pylons and placed his hand on it. Nothing happened at first. Then—

A ripple.

Light surged through the floor rings and into the pylons. The orbs flickered awake, humming with restrained energy. The room responded to Calen's presence like it had been waiting. Aelira flinched as the air thickened with static, the hair on her arms lifting.

Images bloomed in the space between pylons. Not mere projections—these were three-dimensional memories, preserved in crystalline clarity. Figures in regal robes and military garb stood in council, speaking in an ancient dialect. Above them hovered a solar map, hundreds of celestial bodies rotating around a central mass.

"That's not a sun," Aelira whispered, her eyes wide.

"No," Calen breathed. "It's a construct."

The core was not natural—it was artificial, an engineered nexus pulsing with threads of energy. Tendrils of data radiated outward, forming vast pathways through the star systems.

As they watched, the vision shifted, zooming in on a planet near the edge of the system. Nytharis.

Explosions lit its surface. Chaos. A blackened fleet descended like locusts, engulfing cities. Panic spread through the council. The figures dissolved into war.

Calen's heart pounded. "This was a warning system. A record of the fall."

Then, one figure stepped forward in the projection. Its face was pale, marked with the same sigils Calen had seen in his visions.

"Starborn," it said. The voice came not from the hologram but from the walls themselves. Deep. Resonant. Timeless. "If you see this, it means the last seal has fractured."

Calen tensed. "Did it just—"

"—respond to us," Aelira said, her breath caught.

The hologram continued. "The Cradle must be awakened. The Warden sleeps beneath the Shattered Vale. Do not trust the ones who walk in shadow."

Aelira stepped closer, staring at the Warden's name etched in the hovering glyphs. "What is the Cradle? And the Warden?"

"I think," Calen said slowly, "they're parts of the failsafe. From before the Collapse."

The vision dimmed. The energy receded. One by one, the pylons faded, casting the room into silence once more.

Calen stood in the centre, the ancient message still vibrating in his bones. His breath came slow, reverent.

"They knew this day would come," he said. "This whole place was meant for us to find."

Aelira turned to him, her face pale but resolute. "Then let's not waste the warning."

They stepped forward again, deeper into the buried truth of Nytharis.

CHAPTER NINETEEN: THE WARDEN'S THRESHOLD

The corridor beyond the chamber sloped downward like a throat swallowing them into the mountain's dark heart. Its walls, once perhaps sleek and functional, were now wound with twisted conduits and brittle cables—like the fossilized sinews of some long-dead god. The air changed as they moved deeper. It was no longer simply cold; it was aware.

Calen's footsteps slowed, his breathing shallow. The silence pressed in—not empty, but full of *presence*. Something unseen walked alongside them, something ancient and waiting.

The Catalyst, slung at Calen's side, began to tremble faintly. Not violently, but insistently—like a compass needle spinning toward its true north. It tugged him forward with quiet urgency.

Aelira reached for his hand. Her eyes, always sharp, now flicked to the shadows like a hawk scanning for danger. "It's like the air is alive," she whispered. "This place... it remembers."

They descended in silence, their footsteps swallowed by the stone. The corridor opened into a vast atrium carved directly into the mountain's core. Its scale dwarfed them. High above, the ceiling vanished into mist, the stone walls veined with faintly glowing glyphs in hues Calen could not name—colours that shimmered and shifted as though resisting comprehension.

At the atrium's centre stood a cracked pedestal of obsidian-black stone. It was ringed by spiralling glyphs that pulsed like a heartbeat, slow and steady. And above it—suspended within a translucent casing of crystallized vapor—loomed a figure.

It was tall. ARMOURed. Humanoid in shape, but blurred by age and tech. Its features were indistinct, cloaked in layers of energy and mist. Yet its presence was undeniable, like a mountain wearing the skin of a man.

Aelira's breath hitched. "The Warden."

They took a cautious step forward. The air crackled. Static leapt across the stone. The mist enclosing the Warden ignited from within, suffused with eerie light. Then a voice—soft, disembodied, inhuman— slid through the air like silk.

"Starborn… You are not yet ready."

Calen stiffened. The voice had no mouth, no source— yet it rang in his chest like a bell. "Did it just speak?"

A deeper voice followed, layered with ancient resonance, as if rising from beneath the roots of the world itself.

"The Catalyst has awakened. But the burden is not yet yours to bear."

As the words echoed, fine fractures began to spiral across the Warden's crystalline shell. From within came a steady pulse—slow, rhythmic—matching Calen's own heartbeat.

Then came the flood.

Visions slammed into Calen's mind. Cities burning beneath black skies. Ships shattered like glass. A throne of black iron, coiled in smoke and shadow. And on that throne sat a man—his face unmistakable.

His own.

But changed. Corrupted. Eyes rimmed with void. A twisted smile curling lips no longer his.

"No," he gasped, stumbling backward, his balance lost in the wake of the revelation.

Aelira caught him before he could fall. Her grip was firm, anchoring him. "What did you see?"

He struggled to speak, his throat dry. "A path... where I fall. Where I become the thing we're fighting."

Aelira's expression didn't change, but her hand tightened on his arm. "Then don't take it."

The cracking stopped. The light dimmed.

The Warden's voice returned, quieter now, but no less absolute.

"Only through fire is the metal made strong. The Cradle awaits your trial."

Beneath their feet, the glyphs rearranged. The entire floor shifted with a deep, seismic groan, forming a spiral path carved into the stone—leading down into the abyss.

Calen looked into the descending path. For a moment, doubt clung to him like smoke. But then he felt Aelira's presence beside him—her steadiness, her certainty. They had come too far to turn back now.

He took a breath. "No more running."

Aelira drew her weapon, the steel gleaming faintly in the shifting light. She nodded once. "Together."

Side by side, they stepped onto the spiral path, and the threshold of fate swallowed them whole.

CHAPTER TWENTY: THE CRADLE OF FLAME

The spiral path narrowed as it descended, winding like a helix into the bones of the world. The walls shifted with each step—becoming smoother, darker, almost organic. No dust. No decay. Just stone that remembered, lit from within by veins of ancient circuitry that pulsed in slow waves, like the heartbeat of a sleeping god.

Calen's boots scraped softly against the stone, but even the echoes felt subdued, as though the mountain was listening.

The air was hot now—not stifling, but alive. It wasn't just temperature. It was energy. Time. Memory. Every breath carried weight, and each step forward felt like wading deeper into something sacred and dangerous.

The Catalyst at Calen's side no longer tugged but hovered slightly, as if sensing what lay ahead. It had gone quiet, but not dormant. Expectant.

Aelira stayed close, eyes sharp, her sword unsheathed though the hilt trembled faintly in her hand. She wasn't afraid, not for herself—but for him. She could feel the pull in the air, like a tide trying to drag Calen out of reach.

The tunnel opened.

The chamber they entered was vast—cathedral-like, but not in any human design. The ceiling was lost in shadow, flickering faintly with constellations that shifted and realigned of their own accord. The floor was a mosaic of black stone etched with symbols older than language. Heat radiated upward from a central pit that blazed with molten light—neither fire nor lava, but something otherworldly.

A wide ring of obsidian enclosed the pit, forming the forge. But this was no blacksmith's anvil. It was a cosmic crucible.

Hovering above it was a raised dais of translucent material, latticed with gold and inlaid with glowing fragments of crystal. At its centre stood the Cradle—a cocoon of fused glass and energy, gently pulsing with light like the lungs of something waiting to be born.

Calen stepped forward slowly, his voice hushed. "The Cradle..."

Aelira followed, her breath catching. "What is this place?"

The chamber answered.

Not with words, but with sensation. A low vibration thrummed through the soles of their feet and into their bones. A chorus of memory. Grief. Hope. Countless echoes of lives long gone, and of one life yet to choose its shape.

The Catalyst slipped from Calen's belt.

He didn't release it. It left of its own accord—rising into the air like a leaf caught in a silent updraft. It hovered over the pit of molten light, trembling... then began to change.

The weapon folded in on itself, its structure collapsing and reshaping until it became a sphere. Smooth, seamless, radiant. A second sun above a lake of fire.

The forge responded.

Flames rose—but not chaotic. These were sculpted, deliberate. They formed images in the air: a boy alone in the ruins of a shattered colony... a hand reaching toward a dying comrade... a warrior standing before a throne wrapped in smoke. And then—

A man with Calen's face.

But older. Hardened. Crowned by shadow. He stood atop a heap of broken bodies, Catalyst in hand—not as a saviour, but as a tyrant. His eyes were pits of emptiness. His mouth twisted with hunger.

Aelira gasped. "That's not you."

"I don't know anymore," Calen murmured, unable to look away. "Maybe it could be."

The Warden's voice returned—not booming this time, but low and intimate, as if whispered directly into their minds.

"Forge not the weapon—but the will to wield it."

Calen took a step closer. "Then show me."

The flames surged.

They didn't burn his flesh—but they cut deep. Pain lanced through his chest, not physical, but emotional. The fire reached inward, dragging memories to the surface: the hunger in the orphanage, the nights he cried himself to sleep unseen... the first time he realized no one was coming for him. His failures. His fears. The cold voice in his mind whispering that he'd never be enough.

He staggered, fell to his knees.

The fire didn't relent.

"You are *nothing*," the shadow within hissed. "A broken tool. A vessel waiting to be filled by power—or by ruin."

"No..." Calen grit his teeth. He pressed his palms to the forge's floor, trembling. "I'm not a vessel. I'm *me*."

From the fire, a vision rose—Aelira, bathed in starlight, her hand reaching for his. Her eyes held no judgment. Only faith.

Calen reached back.

The flames wavered.

He stood.

Slowly, steadily, the fire coiled around him—not consuming, but transforming. The pain remained, but it no longer controlled him. He welcomed it. Let it temper him.

The Catalyst returned—reshaped, reformed. It settled into his hand, warm and alive. Not a weapon. A promise.

When the light dimmed, Calen stood taller. His armour bore faint new markings—ancient runes etched into the metal. A gentle glow pulsed from his chest like an echo of the Cradle's light. His eyes had changed too—still human, but now they shimmered with the memory of stars.

Aelira approached slowly, wonder softening her expression. "You passed."

He turned to her, eyes bright with quiet fire. "I didn't pass anything. I *chose*. I chose to be more than what I feared. I chose to protect—not because I was born to, but because I *want* to."

The Cradle pulsed once, then grew still.

From the heights of the chamber, the Warden's voice echoed one final time.

"Then rise, Starborn. The final battle awaits."

The forge cooled. The molten light receded. The chamber quieted—not empty, but satisfied.

Calen and Aelira turned together toward the rising path. Behind them, the Cradle faded into stillness once more. Ahead—beyond the stone, beyond the stars—destiny waited, burning on the horizon.

CHAPTER TWENTY-ONE: RETURN TO ZEPHYRA

They emerged from the Cradle's spiral into the outer corridors in silence. The glow from the forge still lingered on Calen's skin like starlight that refused to fade, a quiet heat pulsing beneath his breastbone. Behind them, the great chamber sealed itself without a sound, as if it had simply gone back to sleep.

Neither of them spoke for a time. The mountain had fallen still again, its strange warmth replaced by the chill of stone and memory. But something had changed — not in the air, not in the Catalyst, but in *Calen*.

Aelira's gaze lingered on him as they walked.

"You're different," she said quietly. "Not just stronger. *Settled.*"

Calen exhaled slowly, still adjusting to the silence inside himself. The chaos that had always churned there—the doubt, the fear, the gnawing need to prove himself—was quiet now. Not gone. But *faced*.

"I feel… whole," he said. "Like everything that's ever broken in me has been melted down and reforged."

She gave a small nod. "You were tested. And you chose the harder path."

"Did you know that would happen?"

Aelira paused. "I knew the Cradle wasn't a place of power—it's a place of *becoming*. Only those who are willing to be unmade can come out stronger."

They stopped beneath a low archway, where the last of the forge-light cast their shadows against the wall. Calen turned to face her fully.

"What about you?" he asked. "You've carried this knowledge, this burden, longer than I've even known who I was. What now?"

She didn't answer immediately. Her eyes drifted toward the upper corridors, the way out. "Now... we go home."

Zephyra.

The word hung unspoken between them. Aelira's world. Her people. Her father's kingdom—what was left of it. And the Iron Rebellion, growing bolder with every passing day.

"You think we're ready?" Calen asked.

"No," she said, then smiled faintly. "But we go anyway."

A silence settled between them—heavy, but not unwelcome. There was no triumph in their eyes. Only resolve.

They reached the chamber where they'd first found the Warden's threshold. Now it was quiet again, the glyphs on the walls dim, the pedestal cracked but inert. The mountain had finished its part in their journey.

Aelira knelt, pressed her palm to the stone, and whispered something in her native tongue—an old Zephyrian blessing. Calen didn't ask what it meant. He didn't need to. Some things were meant to be spoken to stone and silence.

Then she rose and turned to him.

"Time to go," she said.

He nodded.

They climbed. Back through the winding halls. Through the whispering dark. Toward the light of the world above.

They stood again beneath the open sky, the mountain behind them like a silent sentinel. The wind was sharp. The stars above burned a little brighter.

Aelira pulled the small emitter from her belt and activated the recall beacon. A low hum pulsed through the air.

"Our ship's still cloaked on the ridge," she said. "Give it a minute."

Calen glanced back at the mountain. "Do you think we'll ever come back?"

"Only if we have to," she said. "Places like this... they don't give without cost."

The ship shimmered into view—sleek, dark, dusted with snow and ash from the wind-scoured ridge. Its engines rumbled to life as the ramp descended.

Calen hesitated at the threshold, then looked at Aelira. "What if I fail?"

She met his gaze without blinking. "Then we fail together."

They stepped inside.

The ship lifted, arcing into the sky. As the mountain fell away behind them, the stars ahead seemed to realign—guiding them home.

And far across the void, the planet Zephyra turned in the dark... waiting.

The ship's hum was a soft constant beneath their feet, like a heartbeat stretched across the stars. They had left the mountain far behind, its silent truths now part of them, folded into the marrow of who they were.

Calen stood at the viewport, watching the void. Stars streamed past like whispers. Zephyra waited ahead— but for now, in this cocoon of metal and light, there was only stillness.

Behind him, Aelira moved quietly. She'd removed the heavier layers of her armour, dressed now in soft flight fabric, her dark hair loose over one shoulder. She approached without a word, joining him at the window.

They stood side by side, not speaking.

Until she said, almost too softly to hear, "You scared me down there."

Calen turned to her. "I scared myself."

She met his eyes, and the silence between them shifted—closer now. Intimate.

"I thought…" She hesitated, then continued, her voice steady. "I thought I was ready to face what came next. The rebellion. The crown. All of it. But the idea of losing you—before we even knew what this is…"

Her words faded, but the meaning lingered.

Calen reached for her hand. Their fingers met, warm and certain.

"You won't lose me," he said. "Not now."

Aelira searched his face, as if confirming it for herself. Then she leaned in and kissed him—softly at first, as though testing something fragile. He returned it without hesitation.

It was not the kiss of victory or hunger.

It was a promise.

They didn't speak as they moved together—past the command console, down the short corridor into the private crew quarters. The walls hummed with the quiet rhythm of the ship, stars drifting beyond the viewport like candles.

Inside, the lights dimmed automatically. Calen paused just long enough to touch her cheek, brushing a strand of hair behind her ear. Her breath hitched—not from uncertainty, but from emotion held back for too long.

Their clothes came away slowly, not urgent, but reverent. Every touch was exploration. Every glance asked, *are you sure?* And each answer was yes.

When they lay together, it was not fire—but warmth. Her skin against his, her body curled beside him like something he'd never realized he was missing. The tension of their journey unwound, breath by breath.

Aelira's hands traced the faint lines of the Catalyst's mark on his chest. "It suits you," she murmured. "This new strength."

"I don't feel stronger," Calen whispered. "I just feel... more alive. With you."

Their movements slowed. Their lips met again—deeper this time, layered with unspoken things:

grief, gratitude, trust, want. And when the final barriers fell, it wasn't conquest. It was surrender.

Later, they lay wrapped in the hush of after. Her head on his shoulder. His hand resting over her heart.

Neither spoke.

They didn't need to.

The stars outside shifted course. The ship adjusted trajectory.

Zephyra loomed ahead—still distant, still shrouded in shadow.

But within that little ship crossing the void, two hearts beat in quiet synchrony.

Ready.

Together.

CHAPTER TWENTY-TWO: ASHES BENEATH STARLIGHT

Zephyra hung like a wounded jewel in the darkness, its surface cloaked in drifting cloud systems and deep violet hues. From orbit, it looked peaceful. But peace was a lie.

Calen stood at the front viewport, eyes fixed on the planet below. He could feel it — a low vibration through the Catalyst, like a distant war drum buried in the earth. Aelira joined him moments later, freshly dressed in her royal combat garb—midnight-blue armour fitted like a second skin, her hair tightly braided, a circlet of polished silver across her brow.

"Home," she said softly.

Calen glanced at her. "Does it feel like it?"

She hesitated, then shook her head. "Not yet."

The ship's console chimed. Atmospheric breach was minutes away. Aelira moved to the pilot's chair, running a diagnostic while Calen slipped into his own armour—sleeker now, marked faintly by the sigils of the Cradle. He'd grown into it. Or it had grown into him.

They descended fast and silent, cloaked from scanners. The atmosphere streaked across the hull in waves of crimson fire before giving way to swirling cloudbanks and the scattered lights of the upper cities.

Calen leaned forward. "Where are we landing?"

"In the old quarter of Lysikar," Aelira said. "It was one of the few zones still loyal to the crown. If any resistance remains… it'll be there."

They breached the clouds.

Below them lay a city once famed for its spiralling towers and vibrant sky gardens. Now, much of it lay in ruin. Buildings still stood, but many were scorched, blackened, pockmarked by skirmish fire. Smoke drifted from the north quarter. The great plaza where Aelira once addressed crowds as a child was eerily silent.

Aelira's voice dropped to a whisper. "They've taken more than I thought."

The ship settled onto a narrow platform behind a collapsed administrative tower. Dust rose around them. No alarms sounded. No patrols came.

Just quiet.

They stepped into the open air. The scent hit Calen first — ash, scorched metal, and something else. Fear. The city held its breath like a creature afraid to move.

Aelira knelt and touched the ground. "There were people here. Recently. Civilians."

"Where did they go?"

She stood slowly. "Or where were they taken."

A shadow flickered across the rooftops nearby.

Calen turned fast, eyes narrowing. "We're not alone."

A low whistle cut through the silence. A moment later, a figure emerged from behind the ruins—hooded, cloaked in dust and wearing the worn insignia of the royal guard.

He approached cautiously, then froze as his eyes met Aelira's. His breath caught.

"Princess?" he rasped.

Aelira pulled back her hood.

"By the stars... you're alive."

More figures emerged—six, maybe seven, all ragged but alert, weapons drawn, eyes wide. One of them wept openly.

The first man knelt. "We thought you were lost. That the bloodline was gone."

Aelira knelt to him, placing a hand on his shoulder. "You kept the flame burning. I swear to you—it's not over."

Calen stepped forward. "Tell us what's happened."

The man stood. "The Rebellion took the capital. They moved faster than we thought possible. The Speaker—he declared the crown dissolved, claimed Aelira had been executed by her own guard. They've locked down the council chambers, seized the communication grid, and started hunting down anyone with ties to the royal line."

"What about the King?" Calen asked gently.

Aelira already knew.

Her eyes didn't flinch. Her voice was steady. "My father?"

The man looked away. "Publicly… they claim he died in exile. But there are whispers. That he's still alive. Being held somewhere underground. Deep beneath the citadel."

Calen felt a shift in the Catalyst—a pull toward the east. Toward danger. Toward something buried.

"We need to move," Aelira said. "I want every loyalist cell contacted. If my father's alive, we find him. If he's gone—we take back what he built."

A slow murmur rose from the guards.

It wasn't cheering. It was *awakening*.

Calen stepped beside her, his voice low. "We light the fires now. And we don't stop until the whole Rebellion sees them burn."

CHAPTER TWENTY-THREE:
EMBERS OF RESISTANCE

The resistance hideout wasn't a command centre. It was barely a shelter.

Buried beneath the shattered remains of a temple in Lysikar's old quarter, it had once been a sanctuary of learning — a place where monks and philosophers had debated the nature of the stars, far from the reach of politics or power. Now, its domes had collapsed, and its prayer stones lay cracked underfoot. Dust drifted through the air in lazy, golden beams, and the light flickered from half-dead power cells wired into exposed conduits.

Yet the space thrummed with something vital.

Hope.

Aelira moved through the narrow corridors with a quiet authority. The rebels she passed stood straighter at the sight of her — but she could read the questions in their eyes. *Is it really her? Has she changed? Can she lead us?* She didn't blame them. The royal line had vanished months ago. Many believed it dead. Some had begun to doubt it had ever mattered at all.

Calen followed a few paces behind, his eyes sharp, taking everything in. These weren't trained soldiers. Most wore civilian garb hastily armoured with scavenged plates. Their weapons were a patchwork of old rifles, stun batons, and smuggled tech. But their eyes... their eyes burned with purpose.

"This was a school once, wasn't it?" Calen murmured.

Aelira nodded. "I came here when I was nine. My father brought me to light the temple fire. I remember thinking it would never go out."

She paused, touching a scorched statue half-buried in rubble — once a scholar with a scroll in hand, now faceless.

"Seems everything burns eventually."

The hallway ended at a wide chamber that had become the resistance's heart. Maps, hand-written reports, and fragmented data-pads littered the stone floor. A table had been constructed from broken columns. Half a dozen resistance leaders gathered around it, rising as Aelira stepped in.

Some stared. Others looked wary.

One, a grey-haired woman with a jaw scar and sharp eyes, stepped forward.

"I'll be damned. It *is* you."

Aelira inclined her head. "Captain Seris. You look well."

"You don't." Her tone wasn't cruel—just honest. "But I suppose none of us do these days."

Another voice cut in — a tall, thin man with a narrow face and a voice like gravel. "If you've come to restore the old ways, princess, you might find your welcome thinner than you'd like. The Rebellion didn't rise in a vacuum."

Aelira met his gaze evenly. "No. It rose from rot. From fear. From cowardice masquerading as justice. I know the crown failed in ways I can't fix. But I'm not here to take back a throne. I'm here to take back *our future*."

Calen stepped forward beside her. "The Iron Rebellion is building something. Weaponizing old tech. They've already seized the council chambers and the comms grid. If they finish whatever they've started, this planet's lost. Not just the crown. All of it."

There was a silence — uncertain, charged.

Then Seris crossed her arms. "And you are?"

"Calen Rourke," he said. "Starborn Catalyst." He paused, then added with a flicker of irony, "Formerly an orphan, wanderer, and general pain in the ass."

A few chuckles broke the tension.

He continued, voice lower now. "I didn't come here for politics. I came here because Aelira risked everything to save this world. And because I saw what's coming."

Another rebel, a young woman with one cybernetic arm, stepped forward. "Coming?"

"They're using *voidtech*," Aelira said quietly. "Old systems. Forbidden for a reason. If they get it stable... they won't just conquer Zephyra. They'll remake it in their image."

The scarred man from earlier frowned. "We've seen shipments heading east—beyond the Black Run. The old mining tunnels. Nobody's touched those in decades."

"That's where they'll be holding him," Aelira said.

"Your father?" Seris asked softly.

She nodded. "If he's alive."

No one spoke. The silence was heavy.

Then Seris stepped forward. "If we do this—if we stand with you—it can't be like it was. No secrecy. No blind orders. We fight *with* you, not *for* you."

Aelira nodded. "Agreed."

Calen added, "And we fight smart. The first step isn't war—it's *unity*. We need every loyalist cell we can reach. Every old connection. Every spark. Before they snuff us out."

Seris looked around the room. The others gave cautious nods.

"I'll put the call out tonight," she said. "Carefully. Quietly."

Aelira exhaled slowly. "Then we start the fire."

That night, in corners of the city no longer patrolled, whispers began to stir. Messages were slipped under doors. Old banners were dusted off and pinned beneath loose floorboards. Tech traders passed coded phrases in crowded markets. A song — once banned — was hummed again in alleyways and shared on corrupted data files.

The Rebellion had the cities.

But the people?

They were beginning to remember.

And far above, in the shattered spire of the capital, a lone figure watched the flickers of light begin to stir in the dark — and smiled.

CHAPTER TWENTY-FOUR: SHADOWS IN THE WEB

The tunnels beneath Lysikar were older than the city itself — predating the Crown, the Rebellion, even the records. Once, they'd carried power and water to temples and knowledge centres. Now, they were dry veins through a wounded body, pulsing only with danger.

Calen moved silently, the dim green glow of his wrist torch catching rusted pipes and collapsed arches. The air was thick with the scent of decay and ozone.

Aelira crouched ahead, her eyes fixed on the motion sensor clutched in her gloved hand. Beside her were two resistance scouts — Kerran, a wiry scout with a mechanical eye, and Vael, a quiet woman with a pulse blade and nerves like steel.

"We're getting close," Aelira murmured.

Kerran tapped a cracked holomap. "The rebels have been using an uplink point in this quadrant. It feeds encrypted comms through the old utility grid — hidden in the architecture. Smart. Took us weeks to trace it."

"And you're sure this is live?" Calen asked.

Vael nodded. "We intercepted a data burst yesterday. Big transfer. It came from somewhere in these tunnels — east arc, sector nine."

Aelira looked to Calen. "If we're lucky, we'll find out what they're building. If we're *very* lucky... maybe we find proof my father's alive."

Calen tightened the strap on his gauntlet. "Then let's make our own luck."

They moved in near silence, steps padded by years of rubble and soot. The deeper they went, the more the walls changed — ancient symbols emerged beneath flaking paint, written in the lost script of the Starborn archives. Some glowed faintly. Others pulsed like warning lights that had waited a thousand years to be seen.

"What is this place?" Aelira whispered.

Calen touched a glyph. The Catalyst stirred faintly at his side.

"Older than Zephyra," he said. "Maybe even older than the Starborn themselves."

They rounded a bend — and stopped.

Ahead, embedded in a wall of collapsed conduit, was the uplink. At first glance it looked like twisted metal — but as they approached, faint lights pulsed beneath the surface. Coils of black fibre, interlaced with flickers of crimson, pulsed like arteries. A central hub throbbed with data activity.

"Voidtech," Calen murmured.

Kerran dropped to one knee, pulling out a relay spike. "I can piggyback their signal. Download whatever they're transmitting."

"You've got two minutes," Aelira said, drawing her sidearm.

Calen stood watch beside her, his senses straining.

It was too quiet.

A moment later, the hub let out a low whine.

"Got something," Kerran said. "Encryption's dense. But I've got file markers — internal troop movements, cargo manifests, something tagged *Subject 0–King*. And something else... a name repeated in fragments."

He looked up, blinking. "They call it *the Hollow Engine*."

Before anyone could ask, a sharp click echoed from the far corridor.

Footsteps.

Aelira raised her weapon. "They're here."

Figures emerged from the shadows — rebels in dark armour, visors down, rifles raised. A squad. Maybe more.

"Go!" Calen shouted. "Get that data out!"

Kerran shoved the spike into a compartment on his belt as pulse fire streaked down the corridor. Aelira dove for cover, returning fire. Vael flanked right, blade gleaming.

Calen didn't duck. He stepped forward, drawing the Catalyst.

Flame burst into the dark — not fire, but radiant energy that shimmered like heat lightning. The first rebel was lifted off his feet, slammed into the ceiling. The rest hesitated.

Big mistake.

Calen moved like a storm. He wasn't reckless, but precise — every strike a dance of flame and light. His blade hummed with power, and the rebels scattered, disoriented.

Aelira took the gap, charging forward with lethal grace, her blade sweeping one attacker aside. Vael took two more before disappearing into the dark.

The skirmish lasted less than a minute.

When it ended, smoke curled in the stale air. The rebels lay stunned or broken. One remained conscious, crawling for his weapon.

Aelira kicked it aside and knelt.

"Where is the King?" she hissed.

The rebel coughed blood. "You'll never reach him. The Hollow Engine is awake. And when it's complete..."

He smiled, teeth red. "Not even the Starborn can stop it."

Then he slumped.

Silence fell again.

Kerran exhaled. "I got the data. It's rough, but I think I can clean it up."

Calen turned, the Catalyst's flame fading. "Let's get out of here. We have answers to find... and war to stop."

Above them, deep within the fortress capital of Zephyra, a new engine stirred in the dark.

It pulsed with stolen power. It whispered to the broken and the damned.

And it waited for its time to rise.

CHAPTER TWENTY-FIVE: ECHOES OF THE HOLLOW

The hideout's main chamber had gone still. The moment they returned, Kerran had locked himself in the comms den — a narrow alcove strung with cables and half-dead monitors. Aelira and Calen stood outside, arms crossed, watching the flickering glow from within.

"He's been in there for three hours," Aelira said, voice low.

"He's trying to crack encrypted voidtech code without an AI core or a decryption frame," Calen replied. "We're lucky he hasn't fried his brain."

A pause.

"He won't stop until he does," she murmured.

Calen nodded, silent.

Through the stone walls, they could hear the resistance base stirring. Word of the ambush had spread fast. Some took it as a sign of boldness. Others... whispered that the Rebellion had eyes even in the dark.

The Hollow Engine.

The name alone chilled the blood. It didn't sound like a weapon. It sounded like a *curse*.

At last, the door to the den opened with a hiss.

Kerran stumbled out, pale, eyes sunken, hands trembling around a blinking drive.

"I decrypted what I could," he said, voice hoarse. "Some of it... it decrypted *itself*."

"What does that mean?" Aelira asked.

"It means," he said, swallowing hard, "the files were alive."

Calen stepped forward. "Alive?"

Kerran handed over the drive. "There's voice data. Audio logs. Internal memos. Whatever this *Hollow Engine* is... it's not just machinery. It *thinks*. And it speaks."

Aelira took the drive gently and slotted it into the base's portable bootable. The lights dimmed. A soft whir. Then projection flared to life.

At first, static.

Then a voice.

Low. Metallic. Worn smooth like a stone in a river.

"Subject 0 resists. Temporal degradation at 43%. Memories remain unstable. Further recalibration required."

Calen flinched. That voice — it wasn't a person. It wasn't even a machine.

It was something *between.*

More static. Then another log.

"Emotional resistance detected. Identity tether remains. Solution: remove anchor. Apply stress test using *Subject Alpha.*"

Aelira's breath caught. "That's me."

Calen turned sharply. "They're *using you* to break him."

Kerran pressed a button. A final log played.

"Reforge the King. Burn the soul. Leave the shell."

The holotable flickered, then shut itself off. The drive smoked — too hot to touch.

They stood in silence for a moment, the shadows around them thick with unspoken dread.

"They're turning him into a weapon," Calen said finally. "Not just a hostage. A *construct.*"

Aelira's face was pale, her voice quiet but steady. "They're trying to erase him. Replace him with something that obeys."

"Voidtech hybridization," Kerran muttered. "I've heard whispers. Projects from the old war. Prototypes that couldn't think for themselves. They broke down. Turned on their creators."

Calen's fists clenched. "And now they're doing it to a *man*."

"Not just any man," Aelira said. "My father. The King."

She looked around the room at the gathering resistance. Vael had entered silently. Seris too. Others stood by, grim-faced and silent.

Aelira raised her chin. "Then we stop this. All of it. The Hollow Engine ends here."

Seris stepped forward. "The question is how."

Kerran wiped his brow. "There's a physical node beneath the Citadel. Old energy distribution system. The logs reference it as a 'containment cradle.' That's where they're holding Subject 0."

"Security?" Calen asked.

"Layered. Biometric, reactive field, likely defended by synthetic units."

"And how long do we have before the process is complete?" Aelira asked.

Kerran hesitated. "One more major sync. Based on the file timestamps... thirty-six hours. Maybe less."

A wave of cold passed through the chamber.

Thirty-six hours.

That was all.

Aelira turned to Calen. "Then we don't wait. We go in. We get him out."

"You'll never make it through the surface defences," Seris warned.

Calen's eyes narrowed. "Then we don't go through the surface."

He stepped toward the map, fingers tracing an arc through the eastern faultline. "We go *under*. The rebels think they've sealed every access point — but the Starborn tunnels run deeper than they know. I saw them... in the Cradle."

Aelira's expression sharpened. "You're sure?"

"I can find them. And if they're still intact... we have a way in."

Seris folded her arms. "A gamble."

"No," Calen said. "A plan."

Later, alone in the quiet just beyond the planning chamber, Aelira stood beneath the shattered roof of the temple's courtyard, staring up at the stars. Her hands trembled, though she kept them clenched at her sides.

Calen approached quietly, the Catalyst's glow a soft flicker.

"He's still in there," she whispered. "I *know* it. And if they take him from me..."

"You won't let them," Calen said.

She turned, eyes glistening. "But what if I'm too late?"

"You won't be."

"How can you be so sure?"

Calen stepped close, placing his hand gently over hers.

"Because the man you're trying to save... raised the woman who brought me back from the dark. And I won't let either of you be lost."

They stood together beneath the stars — two shadows beneath a broken sky, the countdown ticking louder in the silence between heartbeats.

CHAPTER TWENTY-SIX: DESCENT

The entrance to the Starborn tunnels wasn't a gate or a doorway. It was a faultline — a jagged crack beneath a collapsed transit station on Lysikar's eastern edge, half-swallowed by time and dust. From above, it looked like the earth had exhaled and left a wound.

They gathered at first light.

Calen checked the map projection one last time, overlaid with the memory of the path he'd glimpsed in the Cradle — a serpent-like passage curling under the eastern spire, threading deep beneath the Citadel.

Kerran and Vael had packed light. They would go as far as the lower threshold. Beyond that, it would be Calen and Aelira alone.

Too narrow. Too dangerous.

Aelira stood beside him, dressed in reinforced armour tailored to her movement. Her blade rested across her back. Her face was calm, but he saw the storm behind her eyes.

"You good?" he asked quietly.

"I don't need to be good," she said. "I need to be right."

They descended in silence, the narrow entrance giving way to a sloped passage etched with long-faded glyphs. Calen's torch lit the way in flickering arcs of pale blue, but the deeper they went, the more the darkness seemed to push back.

The temperature dropped. The air became still — not stale, but ancient.

Aelira brushed a hand along the wall. "This stone's been untouched for centuries."

"More," Calen said. "This predates the first Zephyrian dynasty. Maybe even the Starborn expansion itself."

She gave a small smile. "Your inner scholar's showing."

He returned it faintly. "It's either that or think about what we'll find at the bottom."

They walked for what felt like hours, following the pulse of the Catalyst. The tunnel split and merged again, forming a labyrinth of smooth curves and sudden drops. Strange symbols flickered faintly on the walls—sometimes glowing, sometimes vanishing when approached.

Twice they passed the remnants of old tech—half-melted panels, dormant conduits, the husk of a sentry unit embedded in a wall like a fossil. Whatever built this place, it hadn't left instructions. Only silence.

Finally, they reached the vault.

It was a chamber of perfect symmetry, round and impossibly smooth. At its centre stood a spire of stone and crystal, spiralling like a frozen flame. Beneath it, a platform shimmered — a transit node, long dead.

Until Calen stepped onto it.

The Catalyst pulsed. The platform lit.

Aelira joined him, tension humming through her stance. "You're sure this will hold?"

"No," Calen said. "But I trust it'll take us where we need to go."

The platform shifted.

No sound. No jolt. Just motion — smooth and dreamlike, like the floor had simply decided to fall.

Darkness swallowed them.

And then light.

They emerged into a different world.

The tunnel here was newer — not in age, but in *corruption*. The walls were veined with metal and obsidian fibre, pulsing with faint red light. The air stank of ozone and cold fire. The floor beneath them was no longer stone — it was grown. Engineered.

Voidtech.

Aelira drew her blade. "We're beneath the Citadel now."

Calen nodded. "This is where they're holding him."

Ahead, the tunnel widened into a gallery — vast and echoing, filled with suspended capsules hanging from the ceiling like cocoons. Inside each one... a form. Some human. Some not. All silent.

"What are these?" Aelira whispered.

Calen approached slowly, gazing into one of the pods.

The occupant inside was a woman. Or had been. Her skin shimmered with synthetic veining, her eyes gone black. No breath. No movement. A flower blooming into ruin.

"Failures," he said. "Test subjects. Fragments of the Hollow Engine's mind made flesh."

Aelira turned to him, jaw tight. "They're *harvesting people.*"

A mechanical hiss echoed from deep within the structure. Then another.

The lights dimmed.

And something began to *wake*.

A low chime pulsed through the corridor.

The Catalyst flared at Calen's side — not in warning, but in resonance.

A whisper, not quite words, filled his mind:

"The Starborn has come. The forge has returned to the fire."

Calen reached for Aelira's hand. "We need to move. Now."

She didn't argue.

They ran.

Through the growing hum. Through the blinking lights. Through the cold breath of machines dreaming in the dark.

They didn't look back.

Because behind them, something ancient stirred.

And ahead... at the heart of the Hollow Engine...

The King awaited.

CHAPTER TWENTY-SEVEN: THE HOLLOW CROWN

The corridor narrowed until it became a throat—organic, pulsing faintly, lined with metal like bone grafted into flesh. Each step forward was met with the soft hiss of unseen machinery, and the low thrum of power surging through veins that should never have been carved into the earth.

Calen felt it in his teeth. In his bones.

The Catalyst burned faintly at his hip, reacting to the wrongness around them. Not fear—but fury.

Beside him, Aelira moved like a drawn blade. Her eyes stayed forward, her posture coiled. She had spoken little since they'd entered the Hollow's deeper layers, but he could feel it—each step was a hammer beat against her heart.

This place was no longer a prison.

It was a *temple*.

And at its centre: the sacrifice.

The corridor ended abruptly at a sealed door—black, seamless, veined with dim red light. At its centre pulsed the sigil of the Rebellion: a burning spiral wrapped in chains.

Aelira stepped forward, placing her palm against it.

The metal hissed beneath her touch, and the symbol rippled—responding to her blood. A final, cruel irony.

The door peeled open like petals of a poisoned flower.

And the chamber beyond was deathly still.

It was circular. Vaulted. Every surface smooth, every light subdued. At its heart stood a platform suspended above a pit of glowing voidlight. And upon it...

A throne.

A man sat there, unmoving.

The air changed. Thickened. Calen felt the Catalyst pulse violently now—not in warning, but recognition.

Aelira stepped into the chamber, eyes wide, heart breaking with every step.

"Father?"

The man stirred.

He was regal in form—tall, broad-shouldered, draped in an ornate fusion of armour and machine. His face was leaner than she remembered, older, gaunt. But it was his. Beneath the layers of augmentation. Beneath the hollow light in his eyes.

"Aelira," he said, but not in greeting.

In *observation*.

Her breath caught. "It's me. I'm here."

The man stood.

Something in his movements was wrong. Too smooth. Too measured. He looked at her the way a weapon might look at its target—calculating. Cold.

"I know who you are," he said. "Subject Alpha. Anchor to Subject Zero's previous matrix. Emotional interference detected."

Calen felt the chill sweep through the chamber.

"No," Aelira whispered. "You're not a machine. You're *my father*. You taught me the old songs. You carried me when I broke my leg on the north cliffs. You said a crown meant nothing if you couldn't bow your head to those who needed you."

The King blinked.

Something in his brow twitched.

Flickered.

"Aelira..." he said, voice softer. "Why are you—?"

The lights above flared red.

A low tone vibrated through the floor.

"ERROR. Subject Zero exhibiting memory deviation. Recalibration required."

"No!" Aelira stepped forward, voice cracking. *"Fight it!* You're still in there!"

The man staggered, one hand pressed to his temple. Sparks flared where his gauntlet met his jaw. The air around him shimmered.

Calen stepped in beside her. "He's still connected to the Engine."

Aelira turned. "Then we *sever it.*"

From the ceiling, tendrils of wire and fibre began to descend—reaching for the man like leeches. He didn't resist.

But *Calen* did.

The Catalyst roared to life in his hand, and he raised it toward the central spire. The chamber reacted—panels sliding back, revealing a web of black conduits converging at a glowing heart: the core node of the Hollow Engine.

"Cut the node," Calen said. "And you cut the control."

Aelira nodded, and without hesitation, leapt from the platform to the surrounding framework. Her blade carved through the first cluster of cables, sending arcs of blue-white light spiralling through the air.

The chamber screamed.

Sparks rained down.

The King fell to his knees, clutching his head.

Calen leapt across the central divide, Catalyst flaring, slicing through the last of the cables feeding the core.

A final pulse burst outward—wave after wave of psychic pressure slamming into them. Visions bled into Calen's mind—Aelira burning. The world crumbling. A throne made of bone.

Then—

Silence.

The chamber dimmed.

The core dimmed.

And the King collapsed.

Aelira was at his side in moments, cradling his head.

His breathing was shallow. His eyes fluttered.

"Father," she whispered.

He blinked. For a moment, just a moment, his eyes were *clear*.

"Aelira..."

He reached for her cheek.

And then his hand fell.

But his chest still rose. Still fell.

"He's alive," Calen said.

"Barely," Aelira breathed.

Behind them, the walls of the Hollow Engine groaned.

They wouldn't have long.

CHAPTER TWENTY-EIGHT: THE GUARDIAN OF IRON

The Hollow Engine groaned around them, a deep, metallic rumble that vibrated through the chamber floor like the growl of a wounded beast. Sparks rained from ruptured conduits, and the cables once tethered to the throne lashed blindly, writhing like dying snakes.

Calen knelt beside the King, helping Aelira ease his body into a stable position. The old monarch's breath came in ragged bursts, eyes fluttering open and shut. Flesh and machine warred within him — torn between man and mechanism.

"We need to get him out," Calen said, voice tight.

Aelira nodded. Her face was pale, streaked with ash and sweat, but her hands were steady. "I'll carry him. You clear the way."

Calen didn't argue.

They moved fast — back across the ruined chamber, toward the corridor that had brought them in. The red glow of the Engine had dimmed to a sullen orange, but something darker stirred beneath the surface. A presence. Watching. Waiting.

The first alarm came as a low chime.

Then the voice — cold, male, synthetic:

"RETRIEVAL PROTOCOL INITIATED. ACTIVATING GUARDIAN."

Calen froze. "That doesn't sound promising."

Behind them, a hatch irised open high in the vault wall.

And something stepped out.

It was humanoid only in silhouette — eight feet tall, plated in segmented iron with voidlight burning beneath every joint. Its face was a smooth, featureless mask of black metal. In one hand, it carried a staff tipped with a spinning blade. In the other, a sphere crackling with kinetic energy.

It didn't speak.

It *charged.*

"GO!" Calen roared.

Aelira darted left, her father slung across her shoulders, moving with inhuman grace even under the burden.

The Guardian moved faster.

It hit the floor with thunderous weight, vaulting the distance between them in a single leap. Its blade swung low — but Calen met it, the Catalyst flashing up in a burst of blue flame.

Steel and starlight collided.

The impact sent shockwaves through the chamber, blowing debris into the air. Calen grunted, staggering under the force, but held his ground. The Guardian was relentless, its blows a machine's rhythm — unyielding, efficient, designed to break.

But Calen wasn't just a fighter anymore.

He *was* the Catalyst.

He ducked low, sliding past a sweeping strike and slamming his palm against the floor. A ripple of energy burst outward, knocking the Guardian back several steps. Not far. But enough.

Aelira had reached the far tunnel. She turned once, watching.

"Calen!"

"I'm right behind you!"

But the Guardian recovered faster than expected.

It hurled the energy sphere.

Calen raised his blade, bracing for impact.

Too late.

The sphere struck just before his feet, detonating in a burst of gravitational force. The floor cracked. Calen was thrown against the wall, the wind blasted from his lungs.

He groaned, coughing dust, vision swimming.

The Guardian advanced.

And for the first time... it spoke.

"STARBORN. DESIGNATION: CALEN ROURKE. FAILURE IS INEVITABLE."

Calen wiped blood from his lip and rose unsteadily.

"Maybe," he said, lifting the Catalyst.

"But I only need to win *once*."

The chamber behind him roared with collapsing metal.

He launched forward, blade igniting.

The final duel began.

In the tunnel above, Aelira paused at a control panel, activating the emergency lift embedded in the old Starborn shaft. The hum of ancient engines came to life — but she didn't relax.

Not yet.

She turned just as Calen burst into the corridor, one arm scorched, blood on his brow, the Catalyst flickering dimly in his grip.

"Where is it?" she asked.

Calen looked back, breathing hard. "Not dead. But buried."

The ground shook as something collapsed far below — iron, stone, and the final shriek of something *not quite alive.*

Aelira hit the lift controls.

The platform rose.

Behind them, the Hollow Engine trembled.

Below them, the Guardian's broken body burned.

CHAPTER TWENTY-NINE: THE HEART OF THE HOLLOW

The floor lurched beneath them, sending a deep, groaning tremor through the metal bones of the Hollow Engine. Red emergency lights stuttered along the ceiling as smoke curled from the walls, the air thick with heat and the scent of scorched circuitry.

Calen caught Aelira's arm as she stumbled, steadying her with one hand and drawing his weapon with the other. Behind them, the rescued King staggered, pale but upright, leaning on the arm of one of the royal guards.

"We need to move—now!" Calen barked over the rising howl of klaxons.

Aelira nodded, eyes sharp, already scanning ahead. The main corridor stretched before them like the throat of a dying beast—its walls pulsing erratically, lights failing, steel groaning under unseen pressure.

"The Heartstone reactor must be destabilizing," she muttered. "This whole place is going to come down on us."

"No doubt a failsafe," grunted the King, his voice dry but iron-willed. "If they couldn't keep me, they'd rather bury me alive with their secrets."

They ran.

Boots pounded on the trembling deckplates as the team tore through the lower access corridor, weaving past collapsing supports and venting steam. Every step forward was a gamble.

Behind them, a detonation shook the complex. A blast door slammed down with a thunderous clang, cutting off one of the auxiliary escape routes.

Calen slammed a fist against the wall panel. "Dead!" he snapped. "Power rerouted. They're collapsing the tunnels behind us."

Aelira's gaze darted to a branching passage. "There's another way," she said. "Maintenance shafts— unmapped, unstable, but they lead up to the dorsal platform."

The King met her eyes. "You know these tunnels?"

"I memorised every schematic while searching for you," she said. "Come on!"

They plunged into the narrow passage, the air growing tighter, the lights dimmer. Overhead, the ceiling cracked, sending sparks raining down.

In the flickering dark, Calen heard something else— movement.

He raised a hand, signalling a stop. "We're not alone."

Shadows peeled themselves from the walls—Iron Rebellion enforcers in blackened gear, armed with shock rifles and grim resolve.

"Go!" Calen shouted, stepping forward. "I'll hold them!"

"Not alone, you won't," Aelira snapped, drawing her blade.

The corridor exploded into chaos. Blades clashed. Rifles barked. The confined space became a warzone of fire, fury, and desperation.

The King, even weakened, found a discarded sidearm and fired with deadly precision, picking off enemies with the cool focus of a man who had once led a galactic fleet.

Aelira ducked beneath a burst of plasma fire and drove her blade through an enforcer's chest, then turned—just in time to see the ceiling crack wide open.

A support beam dropped. Calen threw himself forward, catching her in his arms and rolling them both clear. The beam crashed down where she'd stood.

She stared at him. "You saved me again."

"Always," he said, breathless.

Alarms wailed louder. The walls were trembling like the heartbeat of a dying god.

"This way!" she yelled, guiding them into a narrow side tunnel that climbed like a spine toward the surface.

As they reached the access hatch at the top, Calen keyed in the emergency override. For a moment, nothing happened.

Then the hatch hissed, opened—and the cold night air of Zephyra rushed in.

They emerged into starlight.

Smoke billowed from vents behind them, and a low rumble shook the earth as the Hollow Engine began to collapse inward—imploding with the weight of its secrets.

They turned, side by side, to watch the final ruin of the Iron Rebellion's stronghold.

But even in the wreckage, Calen felt it: a subtle shift, a wrongness in the air. Something had been unleashed.

And it had followed them out.

CHAPTER THIRTY: THE THING THAT ESCAPED

The earth groaned beneath their feet as the last of the Hollow Engine caved in, swallowed by its own collapse. Fire flared from ruptured vents, casting grotesque shadows across the mountainside.

But none of them moved.

They felt it.

A pulse. A whisper. A shiver in the bones of the world.

Calen turned slowly, eyes scanning the darkness beyond the crumpled hatch they had escaped through. The sky above was clear, the stars indifferent. But something had changed.

"What... is that?" one of the guards whispered.

The ground behind them split. A hairline crack, black as void, spread in jagged silence—then widened with a sound like tearing cloth. From it, something slithered.

Not seen—*felt*.

A presence. A pressure. Like a memory wrapped in shadow.

Aelira's breath caught. "It came from the Heart," she whispered. "It was sealed beneath the engine. And we... we set it free."

Out of the fissure, a figure emerged. Vaguely humanoid, but wrong in every way. Its body shimmered, not solid—formed of black glass and flowing mist, like a soul halfway forgotten. Its face was smooth, featureless, save for two eyes that burned with violet fire.

The King took a step back, grimacing. "This is no creation of men. This is... *ancient.*"

"It was imprisoned there," Calen muttered. "Not stored. *Imprisoned.*"

The creature lifted its head, and all sound ceased. The crackle of flames, the distant groans of metal—gone.

Then it spoke. Not with a voice, but directly into their minds. A thousand whispers at once: *You opened the gate. You broke the seal. Now, I remember who I am.*

The air turned to ice.

Aelira stepped forward, sword in hand, but the creature merely looked at her—and the blade in her grasp flared with heat, searing her palm. She cried out and dropped it, her weapon clattering to the rocks.

Calen stepped in front of her, shielding her with his body. "If you want her, you'll have to go through me."

The being tilted its head, curious. *You are touched by the Heartstone... but you are no Catalyst.*

"No," Calen said, his voice steady. "I'm something you'll never understand. I choose who I fight for. And I choose her."

The creature paused—as if considering him. Then it turned its gaze skyward.

I will not fight you... not yet.

And in a breath, it vanished.

The silence returned, and with it, the sound of the burning wreckage behind them.

Aelira retrieved her sword with trembling fingers. "What... *was* that?"

Calen looked up at the stars. "A memory that should have stayed buried."

The King's face was grave. "We need to warn Zephyra. This was not a victory—it was a beginning."

They stood together at the edge of the ruins, the wind cold and bitter around them.

Somewhere in the stars, the creature moved. And it remembered.

CHAPTER THIRTY-ONE: THE GATHERING SILENCE

They rode hard through the mountains under a blood-orange dawn, the horizon smudged with smoke from the Hollow Engine's demise.

No one spoke.

The silence wasn't just exhaustion—it was a silence shaped by fear, by questions unspoken, by the shadow of something vast and ancient that had slipped the bounds of its prison.

At the crest of the ridge, the battered shuttle waited where they had left it, cloaked by the terrain. The pilot, a wiry young Zephyrian with soot on his cheeks, gaped as the party approached—dragging the King, scorched and weary, between them.

"Stars above... You made it," he breathed.

"Just get us in the air," Calen said tightly. "We don't have time."

Within moments, they were airborne, the mountains shrinking behind them. From above, the ruin of the Hollow Engine looked like a wound torn into the crust of Zephyra, still smouldering, still bleeding black smoke.

Calen stood by the observation port, arms folded, eyes locked on the devastation. Aelira came to stand beside him, her face drawn.

"What did we let out?" he asked.

"I don't know," she said. "But I've seen old texts. Warnings, really. The Hollow wasn't just a facility. It was a vault."

"A prison."

She nodded slowly. "The royal archives speak of ancient wars before the rise of the Starborn—battles fought not just with ships, but with… *thought*. With beings that fed on memory, fear, hope. The kind you can't kill—only *contain*."

He turned to face her. "Why would the Rebellion build their stronghold on top of something like that?"

Aelira's expression darkened. "Because they didn't know. Or worse… someone *did*."

Behind them, the King was being tended to by medics. Though weak, he still carried the aura of command. When he caught Calen's eye, he motioned him over.

"I saw it too," the King said quietly. "The thing. The… *Echo*."

"Echo?" Calen repeated.

The King nodded. "That's what they were called, in the oldest records. Echoes of the First War—entities that survived the collapse of the first galactic age. Trapped beneath the surface of worlds, locked behind seals forged in sacrifice. They aren't alive in the way we understand. They're ideas given hunger. And now..."

"Now one is loose," Calen finished.

"And more may follow," the King said grimly. "If one Echo found a crack, others will feel it. The galaxy may not survive a second Awakening."

A heavy silence followed.

Aelira sat beside Calen, brushing a smudge of ash from his cheek. "We saved my father," she said. "But we may have doomed us all."

"No," Calen replied, his voice low but certain. "We didn't unleash it. We just uncovered the truth. And whatever this Echo is—whatever it wants—it won't find Zephyra unguarded."

The shuttle dipped toward the capital, its silver towers gleaming in the distance.

But beyond the stars, something vast stirred.

And it remembered the taste of freedom.

CHAPTER THIRTY-TWO: BENEATH THE STARLIT VEIL

The royal suites were quiet that night, high above the sleeping spires of Zephyra. From the balcony, the city shimmered like a reflection of the stars, distant and fragile in the cool hush before dawn.

Aelira stood at the edge, the breeze tugging softly at her hair. A robe clung loosely to her shoulders, the aftermath of heat and battle still warming her skin. Below, the world slept—unaware of the ancient terror they had awakened beneath the mountain.

Calen stepped into the doorway behind her. He didn't speak. He didn't have to. She felt him there, as constant and grounding as gravity.

"It's too quiet," she said at last, voice barely above a whisper. "It feels like something's waiting to breathe again."

He moved beside her, his presence warm, his gaze cast toward the night. "It is. And so are we."

She turned to him, eyes shadowed by the weight of everything they'd seen. "I'm afraid, Calen."

"Of the Echo?"

"Of losing you."

The words slipped free before she could stop them, and once spoken, they trembled in the air between them.

"I've lived every day preparing to lead Zephyra," she said. "I trained, studied, fought. But nothing prepared me for *you*. And now the thought of facing what's coming—without you…"

Calen took her face gently in his hands, brushing his thumbs across her cheeks. "You won't. I'm not going anywhere. I don't care what that thing was, or what the stars throw at us next. I'm here. Tonight. With you."

She leaned into him, letting her lips find his—soft at first, then deeper, with the kind of urgency that only comes when tomorrow feels uncertain.

They moved together like the ebb and pull of tide, their shared pain melting into something wordless and warm.

Clothes slipped away, lost in the hush of the suite. Skin met skin, not in desperation, but in reverence. They made love with slow intensity, like memorising each other by touch alone.

When they lay still, entangled beneath the silken sheets, the only sound was the rhythm of their breathing—matched perfectly, like hearts that had decided long ago to beat as one.

Calen brushed a kiss to her temple. "Whatever happens," he whispered, "I'm yours. In this life or the next."

"And I am yours," she replied, voice steady now. "No matter the stars."

Dawn spilled golden light across the chamber, soft and warm like the hush between two heartbeats.

Aelira stirred first, blinking against the brightness. Her hand, already resting on Calen's chest, rose and fell with his even breath.

She smiled, listening for a while before she spoke. "Still here?"

Calen cracked one eye open. "I was afraid to blink. Didn't want to wake up alone."

She traced idle circles against his skin. "It's strange. The world's falling apart, and yet this... this feels like the only truth I can hold onto."

He looked at her, serious now. "Then hold onto it. We've already faced death. What's left is to fight for the reason we keep surviving."

She gave him a soft, bittersweet smile. "You're becoming alarmingly wise."

"I blame you entirely."

A quiet knock came at the door.

Duty had found them again.

Aelira sighed, pressing her forehead to his for a moment longer. "The Council's waiting."

"Let them wait five more minutes."

She kissed him once, gently. "Later."

"Promise?"

"With everything I have."

She rose, slipping her robe over her shoulders, her form silhouetted against the morning sun. Calen watched her with quiet awe, the weight of their love grounding him even as the storm gathered once more on the horizon.

Soon, they would face the Echo Council.

But in that brief and golden moment, they were just two people who had found each other in the vastness of a broken galaxy.

And that was enough.

CHAPTER THIRTY-THREE: THE ECHO COUNCIL

The shuttle touched down under cover of darkness, far from the palace, deep in the forgotten belly of Zephyra's old city. Ancient stone vaults and defunct tram lines crisscrossed beneath the capital—a labyrinth of shadows where only trusted loyalists walked.

The King was whisked away under heavy guard, concealed for now. His return would be a rallying cry—but only when the city was secure. For now, the resistance moved like ghosts, threading through the rebel-held streets, avoiding skirmishes, sowing quiet unrest.

Calen and Aelira followed their escort through a rusted maintenance door, past security points manned by grim-faced veterans and oath-sworn guards.

They descended into a chamber carved from basalt and reinforced steel. Torches flickered beside crystalline lights, their glow reflecting off polished stone and faces drawn with weariness.

The Echo Council—or what was left of it—sat in a semi-circle around a table shaped like a broken ring. Each member wore different colours, sigils of their houses, remnants of what unity used to mean.

At the centre sat High Councillor Thale, an aging man with a gaze sharp enough to slice through lies.

He rose. "Princess Aelira. We are told the King lives. Is it true?"

She stepped forward. "It is. He was held beneath the Hollow Engine. We freed him. He's recovering—hidden, for now. But we must act."

"Act how?" asked a younger woman to Thale's right. "The city burns. Rebel banners still fly above the Watchtowers. Your return is not victory."

"No," Calen said, stepping in. "But something worse is coming. Something older than the Rebellion. We didn't just find the King... we released something."

Murmurs spread like ripples in oil.

Aelira's voice was calm but firm. "It was imprisoned beneath the Hollow. A being of thought—of memory and hunger. We call it an Echo. My father knew of it. The Rebellion built their stronghold atop a vault they never understood."

A man to the left scoffed. "You're telling us the Iron Rebellion unleashed a ghost story?"

"No," Calen said sharply. "*We did*—by destroying the Engine. We broke the cage. And now something is loose."

Thale raised a hand to silence the room. "Do you have proof?"

Aelira met his gaze. "Only this—when we escaped, it *spoke* to us. Not with words, but through our minds. It called itself an Echo of the First War."

A silence fell again—but not of disbelief. This time, it was fear.

One of the older councillors, a stooped woman with a scar over one eye, finally whispered, "Then the stars are bleeding again."

Before more could be said, a young officer rushed in, eyes wide. "Forgive me. We intercepted a broadcast."

Thale turned. "From the palace?"

"No. From *him*."

The holo-feed activated in the chamber's centre. A figure appeared—tall, powerful, draped in the Rebellion's blood-and-silver cloak. His hair was short, dark, his jaw sharp, his eyes burning with fanatic fire.

Commander Ryven Drae.

Aelira's breath caught. Her jaw tightened.

Ryven's voice rang out, polished and theatrical. "People of Zephyra. Your King crawls in hiding. Your so-called saviours speak of myths and monsters. I bring truth. I bring *power*. The old world is dying—but a new one rises. One without chains."

Behind him, in the flickering feed, shadows twisted—*watching him.*

Calen whispered, "He knows about the Echo."

Ryven smiled in the projection. "I will meet any who oppose me. Come to the Spire of Flame. Come and see who commands the future of this world."

The feed cut.

Aelira's fists clenched. "He's baiting us."

Thale stood slowly. "He knows you'll come. And he wants to finish what he started. With the Echo behind him."

Calen turned to Aelira. "This is your fight. You said you had to end him."

She nodded once. "I did. And I will."

The room felt colder. The storm they had weathered was only the beginning. Now, the final fire was calling them home.

CHAPTER THIRTY-FOUR: BLOOD OF THE CROWN

The passage to the King's refuge wound through the old catacombs of Zephyra—a place few remembered, and fewer still dared enter. Carved long before the city rose, the walls bore forgotten glyphs and the faint, echoing memories of ancient prayers.

Aelira moved through the dim corridors, her cloak trailing over dust-stained stones, her heart hammering not with fear—but with emotion. She had not spoken to her father since the rescue. Not truly. There had been too many eyes, too much urgency.

Now, it was just them.

She stepped through the final threshold and saw him.

He stood at the far end of the chamber, dressed in a plain tunic, a cane at his side, the crown gone from his brow—but not from his bearing. Even gaunt and pale, **King Alrian** radiated quiet strength.

He turned as she entered. And for the first time since her childhood, he smiled *just* for her.

"Aelira."

Her breath caught. "Father."

He opened his arms, and she crossed the space in an instant, burying herself in his embrace.

They held each other a long while—until words no longer felt impossible.

"You've grown stronger than I ever imagined," he murmured. "And wiser. Zephyra could ask for no better heir."

Tears welled in her eyes. "I'm not ready."

"You are," he said. "I knew it when you came for me."

She pulled back, swallowing the lump in her throat. "We saw it, Father. The thing beneath the Hollow. We thought we were freeing you—but we also set something loose."

His gaze darkened. "An Echo."

"You knew."

"I suspected. I read the sealed volumes in the old archives when I was a prince—tales of entities sealed beneath the crust of ancient worlds. Not creatures. Not minds. Something *other*. The Hollow was built on top of one of the deepest vaults. It was supposed to remain buried forever."

"Ryven knew too," she said. "Or learned enough to think he could use it."

"Then he is more dangerous than I feared."

She hesitated. "He's called us to the Spire of Flame."

He raised an eyebrow. "To parley?"

"To taunt. To draw us out. But I don't think he'll be there. I think it's a trap—and I think the Echo is waiting for us."

The King studied her, then slowly nodded. "Then you must go. But not unarmed. Not just with swords."

He crossed the room and opened a long, iron case— inside, wrapped in starlace cloth, lay a relic: a crystalline dagger, pulsing faintly with white light.

"The *Shard of Vehlan*," he said. "Forged in the last war against the Echoes. It carries part of their sealing magic—pure, untainted."

She lifted it carefully. It thrummed with cold energy in her hand. "Why give it to me?"

"Because I'm too weak to use it now," he said, a sad smile touching his lips. "And because I trust you, daughter. To end what I could not."

They stood together in the stillness of that chamber, two monarchs—one risen, one rising.

"Bring him home," the King said. "Or bring back the fire that will burn his shadow from our skies."

She pressed her brow to his. "I will not fail."

As she turned to leave, the dagger at her side, a whisper followed her:

"Remember, Aelira... the Echo will tempt your heart before it breaks your mind."

She did not look back.

CHAPTER THIRTY-FIVE: THE SPIRE OF FLAME

The Spire of Flame loomed over the ruined eastern quarter of Zephyra like a dagger driven into the earth—jagged, scorched, and defiant. Once a monument to the city's rebirth after the Ember Wars, it had been claimed by the Rebellion in the first wave of the uprising. Now it was a fortress, ringed by automated sentries and banners that snapped red in the wind.

Calen adjusted the scope on his rifle as they crept through the shattered thoroughfares, flanked by a dozen elite guards. Smoke still curled from broken windows. The streets were eerily quiet.

"Too quiet," he muttered.

Aelira crouched beside him, the *Shard of Vehlan* tucked beneath her cloak. Its pulse had grown stronger as they drew closer to the Spire. She felt it in her bones—like a drumbeat buried beneath the skin of the world.

"He's not here," she said at last. "Ryven's not arrogant enough to wait for us in person. He wants us to *think* he is."

Calen nodded grimly. "Then it's a trap. Question is— what's the bait, and what's the teeth?"

They moved forward, slipping past the first line of defences. Inside the Spire, the interior was scorched and gutted, the walls charred black by plasma blasts. Every step echoed too loudly.

"Split team," Aelira ordered. "Five stay at the entrance. The rest with us. Keep comms open."

They moved deeper, past long-dead data nodes and collapsed arches. Then, a sound—faint at first, like breathing through stone.

Then louder.

A *voice*.

You came, as called. So predictable, the flesh-bound.

Aelira froze. "That's not Ryven."

The shadows stirred. The air shimmered.

From the far end of the great hall, a shape emerged— the same *Echo* they had seen at the Hollow Engine, but changed. Larger now. Denser. Its form no longer flickered like smoke—it *commanded* space. Its eyes, twin stars of violet fire, burned into their minds.

Calen stepped forward. "You're not welcome here."

The Echo tilted its head. *I was invited. You broke my chains. Ryven offered me sanctuary.*

Aelira drew the Shard, and it flared to life in her hand, the room bathed in a pale, ghostlight glow. The Echo recoiled slightly.

It hissed—not in fear, but amusement. *Ah. The blade of Vehlan. How quaint. You think me a beast to be caged again? I am memory unforgotten. I am the shadow cast by your ambition.*

"You're a parasite," Aelira said coldly. "Feeding on a world not yours."

I am what your kind buried... and now, I rise. Not through war. Through invitation. Ryven is mine now.

The words hit like thunder.

Calen's jaw tightened. "He's *possessed*?"

No, the Echo said with chilling pride. *He believes. He opened the door willingly.*

Aelira's heart clenched. She had feared Ryven was lost—but not like this. Not *willingly given.*

The Echo surged forward, its form distorting space, a storm of memory and fire.

You came seeking a tyrant. Instead, you face a god reborn.

The guards opened fire. Plasma rounds vanished into the void. Calen launched a charged bolt, but the creature shattered it mid-air.

Aelira gritted her teeth. "Fall back! Don't engage it directly!"

The Echo shrieked—not a sound, but a *feeling*, like heartbreak and betrayal twisted into sound. It ripped through the guards' minds, sending two to their knees.

Aelira raised the Shard and pointed it at the creature. "We will stop you. Ryven will fall. And you will be forgotten again."

No, the Echo said softly. *I have remembered too much to fade.*

And then—it vanished.

Gone in a blink, like a breath exhaled into the cold.

The Spire fell silent.

One of the surviving guards whispered, "What *was* that?"

Aelira's hand trembled slightly as she sheathed the Shard.

"The beginning," she said. "And the warning."

Calen stepped beside her, eyes fixed on where the Echo had stood. "We're not just fighting a rebellion anymore."

"No," she whispered. "We're fighting belief itself."

CHAPTER THIRTY-SIX: WHISPERS AND WARNINGS

They returned to the hidden command post beneath Zephyra as dusk draped its veil across the war-torn skyline. The streets above lay quiet, too quiet—like the world had paused, holding its breath in anticipation of what was to come.

The descent into the catacombs was wordless. No one dared speak—not yet. Not after what they had seen.

The great hall beneath the archives buzzed with muted urgency. Couriers delivered hastily scrawled reports. Tactical officers hunched over holomaps, adjusting formations. The councillors, once sceptical, now whispered in grim consensus.

The *Echo* was no myth. And it had found a voice.

Aelira moved through the murmurs with the Shard of Vehlan still strapped to her side. Its light had faded, no longer pulsing with urgency. That worried her more than she let on. The relic had reacted violently to the Echo's presence—now, it lay dormant.

At the war table, Calen stood beside her, hands pressed against its surface, knuckles white. "He wasn't there. Just that... thing."

"Which tells us everything we need to know," Aelira said. "Ryven is no longer hiding from the truth. He's embracing it."

High Councillor Thale approached, his robes dishevelled, his expression harder than she had ever seen. "Report. All of it."

Aelira gave it to him—every moment, every word. She didn't soften it. There was no comfort in illusion anymore.

When she finished, Thale was silent for a moment too long.

Then: "And you believe Ryven has... *aligned* himself with this being?"

Calen folded his arms. "It told us plainly. He *invited* it. Willingly."

"That's impossible," said Councillor Meris, a sharp-featured noblewoman nearby. "No one would—"

"Fanatics would," Aelira cut in. "Especially when cornered. He's losing control of the city. The King has returned. The Hollow is gone. He needed a new weapon. One we can't easily fight."

An officer rushed in from the upper corridors, breathless. "Intercepted chatter, Councillors. Rebel cells are consolidating forces across the inner ring. But that's not the worst of it—"

He passed Thale a datapad. The old man scanned it, his face paling slightly.

"They're not just gathering forces," he said. "They're... constructing something. A device. A *conduit*. Located at the Sanctum Apex."

Calen leaned closer. "Purpose?"

"Unknown," the officer replied. "But preliminary analysis of the site suggests a massive energy lattice. Ritualistic layout. Crystalline channels—reconstructed from old, forbidden texts."

Aelira's blood chilled. "They're building a gateway."

"To what?" Calen asked.

She shook her head. "Not to another *place*. To another *state*. They're preparing a vessel."

Thale looked up slowly. "To *host* the Echo."

Aelira turned away, running a hand through her hair. "He's not just submitting to it. He's preparing to become it. He's letting it into his flesh, into the bones of the city."

Another silence fell, heavier this time.

"We need to strike now," Calen said. "Destroy the conduit before they complete it."

Thale was grim. "It's not that simple. They've embedded it deep within the oldest temple—layers of shielding, rebel guard rotations. It's practically a fortress."

"Then we infiltrate," Aelira said. "A small team. No war drums, no grand charges. Just shadow and steel."

Thale studied her carefully. "You intend to go yourself?"

"I have to," she said. "This is my city. My burden. Ryven was once my greatest ally—my greatest *friend*. I can't ask anyone else to face what I must."

Calen stepped forward, resolute. "Then I go with you. No arguments."

She didn't argue.

Instead, she looked at Thale. "We'll need schematics. Intel. Supply caches inside the perimeter."

"You'll have them," Thale said. "And the blessing of every loyal heart left in Zephyra."

As the Council dispersed to prepare, Aelira turned to Calen, her voice low. "This conduit—it won't just draw the Echo. It will *anchor* it. If they finish it, we'll be too late."

Calen nodded. "Then we stop it before the first stone sets."

Aelira touched the hilt of the Shard. It vibrated faintly—awake again.

She closed her eyes.

Let this be the last descent into darkness.

CHAPTER THIRTY-SEVEN: THE CONDUIT

The moon hung low over Zephyra, pale and watchful. Down in the inner ring, the city's oldest quarter—once home to scholars, temples, and philosophers—was now shrouded in darkness, lit only by flickering torchlight and the sharp white beams of rebel patrols.

Calen and Aelira moved like ghosts through the ruins, cloaked in silence, every breath timed to the rhythm of distant footfalls. Around them, the remnants of an ancient world loomed—arches carved with star-scripts, statues of long-forgotten guardians now cracked and moss-covered.

But beneath the beauty, something *wrong* pulsed in the stone.

The *conduit* was nearly complete.

They had seen the blueprints. The rebels were following patterns not of their own design, but *replicated* from ancient glyphs—drawn from Echo relics scattered across the void. Crystalline spires jutted from the Sanctum Apex like teeth, forming a jagged circle around a hollow platform of obsidian.

At its centre, suspended by invisible force, was a black sphere—*not quite matter, not quite light—*turning slowly like a heartbeat.

Aelira ducked behind a fractured column, peering through her scope. "They've embedded the core already. That sphere... that's a focus. They're preparing to *feed* it."

Calen slid in beside her. "Guards on every tier. Sensors. Auto-turrets. But no heavy artillery. They're guarding something delicate."

"Because it's *alive*," she whispered. "It's not just tech. That thing is *listening*."

He glanced at her. "You feel it too?"

She nodded. "It's not just looking for a vessel—it's *choosing* one. And Ryven's offering himself."

From the east, two more rebels entered the chamber below, carrying crystalline components—shaped like antennae or tusks. They inserted them into sockets along the perimeter. The black sphere pulsed in response.

Aelira flinched. "It's accelerating."

They had minutes—maybe less.

"Diversion?" Calen asked.

She shook her head. "Too loud. We need to disable it from within."

She pulled a small device from her belt—a disruptor beacon laced with anti-phase charges. "If I plant this at the sphere's base, we can destabilise the lattice. It'll implode the conduit."

"And the guards?"

"I'll get in. You cover me. No alarms. No heroics."

He gave her a long look. "No dying either."

A faint smile. "You first."

She slipped into the shadows, moving like liquid silver. Every motion was precise, every breath controlled. She scaled a broken support column and dropped silently into the central tier, heart pounding like a drumbeat in her ears.

The Echo's presence pressed against her thoughts. She could feel it whispering—not in words, but in *feelings*: belonging, power, destiny.

It was seductive.

But she kept her focus.

Calen watched her from above, rifle ready, tracking every movement. When a guard stepped too close, he exhaled once—and fired a silenced round. The rebel dropped without a sound.

Aelira reached the core.

The sphere hung before her, spinning slowly, black and endless. As she approached, the Shard of Vehlan burned at her side—glowing white-hot.

The Echo spoke.

You could be more than queen. You could be eternal.

Her hand trembled—but she placed the disruptor at the base.

"Not today," she whispered.

She activated it—and ran.

The pulse was immediate. A soundless wave tore through the air, shattering the crystal veins and causing the sphere to flicker wildly.

Rebel guards turned, shouting. Sirens flared.

Calen fired again and again, clearing her path.

Aelira leapt from the central platform just as the sphere buckled inward.

The explosion was strangely quiet—like the void inhaling. The sphere collapsed into itself, taking the conduit with it in a crackling scream of light.

The blast threw her sideways. Calen caught her mid-fall, his arm wrapping around her as they crashed behind cover.

Then—silence.

And a ripple.

Not of air. Not of sound.

Of *space.*

From the smouldering heart of the sanctum, a shape *stepped forward*. Not Ryven. Not human.

A manifestation. Not fully formed, not yet—but close. A shape sculpted from memory, bone-thin, impossibly tall. The Echo had touched the threshold—and had *begun to walk*.

It turned its burning eyes on them.

You delay the inevitable. But you cannot stop the tide.

And then it vanished.

Not destroyed. Not defeated. Just *waiting*.

CHAPTER THIRTY-EIGHT: THE TIDE UNLEASHED

The old stone chamber beneath Zephyra's palace walls had once been a war chapel—its arched ceilings blackened by the candles of a hundred generations. Now it served as a makeshift command room, lit by flickering holos and the quiet voices of those still fighting to save the city.

Aelira sat on the edge of the war table, her cloak draped loosely around her shoulders, eyes fixed on the faint burns across her gloves. The Shard of Vehlan rested beside her, dulled after the conduit's collapse but still faintly pulsing—like a heartbeat keeping time with the danger still out there.

Calen stood at the opposite end of the table, speaking in low tones with Thale and the King. The others moved around them like shadows—officers, scouts, messengers carrying words that were beginning to turn from fear into something else.

Resolve.

The destruction of the conduit hadn't broken the rebellion—it had galvanized the people. News had spread. The Princess had struck at the heart of Ryven's new power, and she had *survived*.

The streets were stirring.

But the Echo had *not* been destroyed. And that truth lingered in every breath.

King Alrian moved toward her, a subtle limp in his step, but his presence undiminished. He sat beside her in silence for a moment, watching the flickering shadows across the stone floor.

"You did well," he said at last.

Aelira didn't answer immediately.

"There was a moment," she said. "When I reached the core. I could hear it. It didn't speak in words, but I *understood* it."

He nodded solemnly. "That's how it begins. That's how they twist the soul—by offering something your heart already longs for."

She turned to him. "It offered me eternity. Power. Peace. It promised I'd never have to lose again."

"And you said no," he said. "That is the greatest victory of all."

She looked away. "I'm not sure I said no because I was strong. I think I said no because Calen was watching me."

The King's smile was faint, but proud. "Then thank the stars for love, child. Even the ancients never found a weapon stronger."

Across the room, Calen caught her gaze and nodded once. Just a look—but it said everything.

Thale approached, a datapad in hand. "We've decoded part of the relic pattern used in the conduit's construction. It's incomplete—but the structure matches something from our most forbidden archives."

He paused, then tapped the pad.

The image shifted—an ancient sigil, composed of interlocking rings and broken stars.

"The *Mouth of the Hollow Star*," he said. "A gate used only once, during the First Collapse. It was said to allow not travel—but *transcendence*. The body changed. The mind overwritten."

Aelira's stomach turned. "They're not just letting the Echo in. They're building it a *permanent host*."

Thale nodded grimly. "And Ryven is offering himself as the foundation stone."

The King rose, his voice gaining strength. "Then this is no longer a rebellion. This is a *possession*—of city, of body, of history."

He turned to his daughter. "And it must end with fire."

Calen stepped forward. "We need to draw him out—before the transformation completes."

Thale's eyes narrowed. "How?"

Calen looked to Aelira, and for the first time, she saw in him a flicker of something dangerous.

"We don't go after Ryven," he said. "We make him come after *us*."

CHAPTER THIRTY-NINE: THE BAIT AND THE BLADE

The war room had grown quiet. The maps no longer flickered with movement. The updates had slowed to a crawl. All that remained was decision.

Aelira stood with her hands braced on the stone edge of the war table, the Shard of Vehlan resting at her hip like a sleeping serpent.

Calen paced behind her, quiet but coiled. Across from them, King Alrian sat, one hand resting on his cane, the other tapping the table in slow, thoughtful rhythm. Thale stood beside him, a datapad in hand, watching Aelira like a man bracing for the wind.

"We can't keep reacting," Calen said at last. "The conduit wasn't the end—it was the *opening volley*. Ryven's not finished. The Echo's got its claws in him now."

"And its eyes are on her," Thale said, nodding toward Aelira.

She didn't flinch. "Because I'm the last thread Ryven didn't unravel."

"Exactly," Calen said. "He's not just fighting a war— he's building a legend. You're the part he didn't conquer. So we use that."

Aelira raised an eyebrow. "You want to use *me* as bait?"

"You'd be the sharpest bait in history," Calen said with a faint grin. "We send a message. A challenge. From you. Broadcast to every rebel cell, every hidden transmitter. Make it public. Make it *personal*."

Thale's brow furrowed. "And if he knows it's a trap?"

"He *will* know," Calen said. "That's the point. But the Echo won't let him walk away from it. It feeds on confrontation. It thrives on emotion. He'll *have* to answer."

Aelira turned to her father. "We call him out. Publicly. No armies. Just me. On sacred ground. The Citadel ruins."

The King leaned forward, his gaze sharp. "And he comes alone?"

"We *say* alone," Aelira said. "But we prepare for war. We hide strike teams in the ruins. Cut off retreat paths. Blind his tech with disruptor fields. When he's isolated, we end this."

Silence stretched between them.

Finally, the King stood. "A bold plan. Reckless. But it may be the only way to draw him into the open. If we don't stop this now, there won't be a Zephyra left to save."

"I'll do it," Aelira said. "He was once my mentor. He taught me to fight. Now I have to show him what he created—and what he *couldn't* break."

Calen stepped beside her. "You're not facing him alone."

She met his eyes. "I have to."

"No," he said, quietly but firmly. "We go in together. You may carry the crown, Aelira, but I carry *you*."

Her protest never left her lips. Instead, she nodded.

Thale stepped forward, voice hushed. "I'll write the message. Clean. Short. Direct."

He tapped out the words, then looked up. "We'll broadcast it on every rebel frequency in the city."

Aelira looked at the recorder before her. Her heart was steady. Her resolve, stone. She activated the channel.

"This is Aelira Vaelori of House Zephyra. Daughter of the Crown. Heir to the flame."

"I offer no apology for surviving. No shame in defending my people. But I offer a choice."

"Come to the Citadel ruins at dawn, Ryven. No armies. No Echo. Just you and me."

"Let's finish what we began—face to face. Flesh to flesh. Or show the galaxy what you've become: a coward in the skin of a king."

She closed the channel.

Silence.

Then Calen whispered, "He'll come."

"Oh, yes," the King said, straightening. "The only thing greater than power... is the need to prove you still deserve it."

Far away, in the depths of the rebel-held zone, a shadow twisted as it heard the broadcast. The Echo had no mouth—but it smiled.

The time was almost right. The vessel was nearly ready.

And the flame would soon meet the hollow.

CHAPTER FORTY: THE EDGE OF DAWN

The ruins of the Citadel lay quiet under the bruised light of false dawn. Shattered marble columns cast long shadows across the cracked flagstones. Once, this had been the seat of Zephyra's wisdom and law. Now, only silence remained—thick, expectant, like the breath before a scream.

High on the northern terrace, Aelira stood alone, overlooking the courtyard where her challenge had been set. The wind tugged at her cloak, and the Shard of Vehlan gleamed at her side like a sliver of frozen starlight.

Behind her, Zephyrian elite waited in silence—hidden in the fractured bones of the old towers, watching from high walkways and behind collapsed walls. Precision teams. No banners. No fanfare. Only resolve.

Calen approached quietly. He stopped a few paces behind her, watching her silhouette against the rising light.

"You've barely moved in an hour," he said.

"I'm listening," she replied.

"To what?"

She turned her head slightly. "To the city. It's breathing differently today. As if it knows what's coming."

He stepped beside her, his voice soft. "You sure he'll come?"

"He'll come," she said. "He has to. There's no throne for him unless I fall. No audience unless he answers the challenge."

Calen studied her for a long moment. "You've changed."

She looked at him, a small, sad smile forming. "So have you."

He nodded slowly. "I think that's what scares me. That this ends with one of us changed into something we can't come back from."

She reached for his hand, and their fingers laced without hesitation.

"If we don't change," she whispered, "then we didn't survive."

Below, a rumble echoed through the courtyard. Engines—moving slow. Deliberate.

A transport slid into view, flanked by dark-armoured soldiers. Too few for an invasion. Enough for theatre.

The transport stopped.

A lone figure stepped out.

Clad in a crimson mantle, armour like obsidian glass veined with flickering lines of violet light, **Commander Ryven Drae** walked forward as though time had never passed.

But it had.

And his eyes no longer belonged to him.

Aelira's grip on the Shard tightened. "He's already begun the binding."

Calen's voice was low. "Then this isn't just a duel."

"No," she said. "It's an exorcism."

The sun broke the horizon at last, light spilling across the ruins.

From the shadows, the Echo stirred—watching. Waiting.

And on the edge of dawn, fate stood poised to strike.

Ryven walked with the calm of a man who believed he'd already won.

Every step echoed across the courtyard, boots crunching softly on ancient stone. The crimson of his cloak trailed behind him like a spill of blood, and the twisted shimmer of the Echo's influence clung to him—subtle at first glance, but undeniable.

His once-proud features had grown sharper, hollower. His eyes, once fire-forged and full of purpose, now gleamed with something colder—detached, *other*.

Aelira took a step forward, letting go of Calen's hand. She moved with poise, with grace, with steel in her spine.

Ryven stopped a dozen paces away.

"Aelira," he said. His voice was unchanged—rich and steady—but behind it, something whispered.

"Ryven," she replied evenly. "Or whatever remains of him."

He smiled faintly. "Still with the blade on your hip and fire in your voice. I wondered if the girl I trained would survive the war."

"She did," Aelira said. "But the man who trained her didn't."

Ryven tilted his head, almost curiously. "I transcended him. That man was limited by law, tradition, and sentiment. I am none of those things now."

"You're hollow," she said. "And you've mistaken it for ascension."

He chuckled. "Is that what this is? Your grand retort? Your final stand? Words and nostalgia?"

"No," she said. "This is a reckoning."

Ryven's gaze slid past her, toward the ruins. "How many of your loyalists are hidden among the stone? Twenty? Forty?" He shook his head with mock sadness. "It won't matter. The moment I fall, the Echo will rise. The world is already shifting. Your Empire is already crumbling."

"You're not an empire," Aelira said. "You're a wound that forgot how to heal."

At that, something flashed behind Ryven's eyes. For a heartbeat, she saw him—the real man. The one who once swore oaths beside her father. The one who once laughed during training, who believed in unity, in Zephyra.

But then it was gone. Swallowed by violet fire.

"The time for talk ends," he said. "Let's see what the last light of Zephyra can do."

Aelira drew the Shard.

It burst into flame.

The air shifted—tense, tight, *ready*.

And high above, the Echo leaned closer.

CHAPTER FORTY-ONE: DUEL OF THE HOLLOW FLAME

The wind stilled. The stone held its breath. Even the sun, casting its light across the ruins, seemed to dim.

Aelira stood with the Shard of Vehlan in hand, its white flame dancing along the blade—pure, bright, and alive. Before her, Ryven raised a weapon of his own: a jagged sword wrought of black metal and violet light. It pulsed unnaturally, humming with the rhythm of a heartbeat that was not his own.

The Echo was inside it. Inside *him*.

They circled each other slowly, feet brushing ash and sand.

No more words.

The first clash came sudden as lightning—Aelira moved with precision, driving forward, her blade meeting Ryven's in a brilliant flare of light and shadow. The shockwave cracked the stone beneath them, sending dust rising like smoke from old altars.

Calen, watching from above, didn't breathe. The others stayed still, hands gripping triggers, but none dared interfere. This was not a battle of armies. It was a battle of souls.

Ryven struck again, his blade swinging in an arc like a guillotine. Aelira ducked beneath it, rolled, came up fast, and slashed across his shoulder—her blade hissing as it touched his armour.

He stumbled.

But the wound didn't bleed.

It glowed.

The Echo's energy pulsed through him, sealing the gash, reinforcing his frame. He laughed—low, echoing, distorted.

"Did you think I'd bleed for you?"

"I don't want your blood," Aelira said. "I want what's left of *you* to hear this."

She pressed the attack. The Shard moved like liquid fire, striking with elegance and force. Ryven met her, blow for blow, power for precision. The air rang with every impact, the very ruins seeming to shake beneath the strain.

"You still believe in mercy," he sneered, locking blades with her. "You still believe there's something to *save*."

Her eyes locked with his. "I don't believe it. I *hope* for it."

For a moment—just one—his grip faltered. His sword dipped.

And Aelira struck.

The Shard drove deep into his side, burning through armour and shadow alike. He roared—not in pain, but in defiance. His other hand shot out, grasping her throat.

"You think this ends me?" he growled. "You think the Echo will just *let* me die?"

The world shuddered.

The sky turned a shade darker.

The ground beneath the Citadel cracked—black veins spiderwebbing outward.

From Ryven's mouth, a second voice spoke—ancient, layered, and *cold*.

If this shell fails... I will take hers.

The Echo reached for her.

But the Shard flared *brighter*. A light that was not heat—but memory. Love. Honor.

The voice screamed.

Aelira twisted the blade and drove it upward.

Ryven staggered back.

The Echo peeled away from him like smoke in a gale—screaming, writhing, *fractured*.

And Ryven collapsed.

The light faded.

The ruins stood still once more.

Calen ran to her side. She dropped to her knees, trembling, not from exhaustion—but from the sheer force of what she had just survived.

Ryven lay gasping, his eyes no longer glowing.

"I... was so sure..." he whispered. "I thought it would save us..."

Aelira knelt beside him. "It wasn't saving you. It was *consuming* you."

His eyes fluttered. "I see it now... I see it all..."

He reached for her hand.

She took it.

And in that final moment, Ryven Drae died—*not* as the Echo's vessel, but as the man he once was.

The wind picked up again.

The city breathed.

And in the distance, the faintest tremor echoed—*the Echo still lived*.

Wounded. Shattered. But not yet destroyed.

CHAPTER FORTY-TWO: ASHES AND AFTERMATH

The sun climbed higher over the Citadel ruins, casting long, broken shadows across the scorched ground. Smoke still curled from the fractured flagstones. The wind carried ash like snowflakes, grey and soft, too gentle for what had just transpired.

Aelira knelt beside Ryven's body, his hand still caught loosely in hers. His face was peaceful now. The cruel rigidity had faded from his features, leaving behind something painfully human.

She had wept, but not for his death. She had wept for the man she remembered—the brother-in-arms, the teacher, the firebrand who once stood beside her father to rebuild Zephyra from the ashes of old wars.

That man had died long before today.

Behind her, the soldiers emerged in silence. No cheering. No shouts of victory. Just the hushed movement of boots across stone and the faint clicking of comms as reports were whispered across the city.

The rebellion was crumbling.

But something worse remained.

Calen stood watch beside her. His rifle was slung across his back, unused since the first clash. He hadn't needed it. Her duel had become something sacred—something he would not desecrate.

"She didn't scream," he said quietly.

Aelira looked up at him. "Who?"

"The Echo," he said. "When you drove it out. It didn't scream in pain. It screamed in *anger*."

She nodded slowly. "It wasn't dying. It was *denied*."

Footsteps approached. King Alrian, flanked by Thale and a few councillors, walked slowly into the broken courtyard. The King's eyes passed over Ryven's body, then to his daughter.

Aelira stood, slowly and with dignity. Her face was pale, but unshaken. "It's done."

Thale looked at Ryven's corpse with no joy. "I remember when he swore loyalty to your father. His voice carried through these halls like a war-horn. How far he fell."

"He didn't fall," Aelira said softly. "He was *taken*. Piece by piece."

The King studied her. "And what of the Echo?"

"It withdrew," she replied. "Not defeated. Not destroyed. It... left."

Thale frowned. "You mean it escaped?"

"No," Calen said. "It *let* us win."

The council chamber grew still.

Thale brought up his datapad and hesitated before speaking. "We've been monitoring the tectonic scans since the conduit's collapse. There's... movement."

He turned the pad to show them.

A heat signature pulsed deep below Zephyra. Not a creature. Not a weapon. A *pattern*. Vast. Circular. Pulsing like a heart.

"It's not gone," Thale whispered. "It's *growing*."

The councillors murmured, shaken.

"It's preparing something," Aelira said. "Another vessel. Or worse."

The King turned toward the north, toward the horizon. "Then this wasn't the final battle. This was the opening of a deeper war."

Aelira's hand found Calen's. She gripped it, tight.

"Let the world think today was our victory," she said. "We'll let hope rise."

"And while it rises," Calen finished, "we'll go beneath."

CHAPTER FORTY-THREE: THE HEART BELOW

The entrance to the forgotten tunnels was nestled beneath a collapsed stairwell in Zephyra's oldest quarter—a place older than the rebellion, older than the King's reign. Older, perhaps, than memory.

Aelira stared into the void below. A ragged hole opened between crumbling stone, its mouth lined with ancient bricks that bore no mortar, no binding—only pressure and age holding them together.

The scent that wafted up was not rot. Not damp. It smelled like *dusty thought*. Like a memory too long left alone.

Calen stood beside her, torchlight flickering off the matte plates of his armour. "Tell me again why we're the ones going into the pit of forgotten nightmares?"

"Because no one else would come back whole," she said quietly. "And we might."

Behind them, Thale checked the seismic map once more. The pulse they'd seen on the tablet radiated from beneath this precise location, almost as if it were *timed*. Every thirty-four seconds, a low vibration rippled through the ground, like the heartbeat of something buried but dreaming.

The King had given no direct order. He hadn't needed to. His last glance at his daughter before she descended had said enough: *Go find the truth, whatever it costs.*

They descended in a group of five: Aelira, Calen, and three hand-picked scouts—Loran, Idris, and Kessa. Veterans. Each had served in battles where silence was a weapon and nerves were the first to die.

The first steps were simple. A crumbling stairwell spiralled downward through fractured stone. Torches lit the way with trembling light, their beams swallowed too quickly by the thickening dark.

After fifty feet, the stone changed.

"What is this?" Kessa asked, brushing her hand against the smooth tunnel wall.

Calen crouched beside it. "This isn't quarried."

"It's *fused*," Aelira said. "Melted and reshaped."

The temperature dropped as they pressed on—not with cold, but with emptiness. The kind of emptiness that made your bones feel too light.

And then the symbols began.

Carved into the walls in spirals and sweeping arcs, the glyphs glowed faintly—like veins beneath thin skin.

Calen stared at them, frowning. "They look like writing, but they... shift. I can't focus on them."

"Don't try," Aelira murmured. "They're meant to draw thought out of you. To replace it."

Further in, the path opened into a vaulted chamber—vast and silent. The floor was seamless, black stone. The ceiling arched overhead, supported by ribbed columns that pulsed faintly in time with the vibrations.

At the centre stood the structure.

A spire of living crystal, spiralling upward like a frozen scream.

It beat.

A soft *thump-thump*, like a heart under flesh.

Aelira stepped forward slowly, the Shard of Vehlan pulsing at her hip. "This is the source."

Calen followed, his voice hushed. "Is it a machine?"

"No," she whispered. "It's *becoming* one."

The spire wasn't alive—but it was awakening. And not on its own.

From the walls, dark strands of energy flickered and flowed inward, drawn like threads to a central weave.

Idris raised his scanner. "It's absorbing thoughts. Memory. That's why it's here—beneath a city full of minds."

Loran muttered, "This isn't a hiding place. It's a feeding ground."

Aelira's hand touched the base of the spire. It was cold—and yet it trembled beneath her fingers.

A whisper brushed the edges of her mind. Not a word. A *presence*. Curious. Watching.

Calen pulled her back. "Did it touch you?"

She nodded slowly. "Only enough to recognise me."

"Recognise you?"

"I don't think we found it," she said. "I think it was waiting for *me*."

A silence fell between them.

And then, the pulse grew stronger.

The floor shivered.

The glyphs brightened.

A low hum began—deep, harmonic.

The Echo was *stirring*.

And whatever slumber it had been in—it was ending.

CHAPTER FORTY-FOUR: THE BECOMING

The pulse quickened.

It wasn't a sound anymore. It was *within them*—a beat beneath their hearts, a tremor behind the eyes, a strange, low pressure that built like a storm against bone.

Aelira drew the Shard of Vehlan slowly, and it flickered in her hand—not with fire, but with a dull, wavering glow. It pulsed out of sync with the rhythm around them, as if the relic were resisting an invisible tide.

"We need to move," Calen said, scanning the vaulted chamber. "There's something in the air. Can you feel it?"

Aelira nodded. "It's not just awakening. It's *searching.*"

The walls breathed. Not literally—but they seemed to expand, contract, pulse with the same rhythm as the spire. The glyphs moved subtly now, tracing slow, sinuous paths like ink bleeding across skin.

Then came the shift.

Subtle.

Terrible.

Aelira blinked—and she was *elsewhere*.

No sound. No warning.

She stood in the courtyard of the royal palace, years ago. The air was warm, heavy with summer jasmine. A child's laughter rang out across polished stone.

Her own voice.

And across the courtyard stood her mother, alive and smiling. Arms open.

"Aelira," the queen whispered. "Come here, my starlight."

Her heart cracked.

She took a step.

Then stopped.

Because her mother's eyes *weren't her mother's eyes.*

They were violet.

The smile widened—too wide. Her mother's voice dropped, layered over by another, older voice:

"Even grief is a door."

Aelira staggered. The memory fractured.

She gasped—and she was back in the chamber, one knee on the ground, sweat slicking her brow. The

Shard had dimmed to a glow no brighter than a dying ember.

Across from her, Kessa had dropped her torch and was clutching her head. "He's whispering," she cried. "He's *in me*! I see my sister—I see her face—but it's not *her*! It's *him!*"

Calen moved fast, grabbing her by the shoulders. "Stay with me. What do you see?"

Kessa blinked rapidly, breathing like she was drowning. "She's telling me to let go. To let the pain end. To *join* her. She says... she says I don't have to be afraid anymore."

"It's lying," Calen said gently. "It's not your sister. It's *never* her."

Behind them, Idris stood still.

Too still.

Aelira turned. "Idris?"

He didn't answer.

His head tilted unnaturally.

And then he smiled.

The voice that came from him was not his own.

"Catalyst. Crown. Flame. Thread. You weave yourselves so tightly. Let me show you how quickly threads can snap."

His hand raised—and *glyphs along the walls flared.*

Aelira raised the Shard. "Idris! Fight it!"

The Echo didn't flinch. It used his voice like a marionette's strings.

"He let me in. You all do, eventually. Even in your brightest memories, you ache. And I am ache made whole."

Kessa sobbed, reaching for Idris—but Calen caught her arm.

"Don't."

Idris stepped forward—jagged energy dancing across his limbs. The glyphs responded, brightening with every word he spoke.

The scouts were frozen.

And then, Aelira moved.

She plunged the Shard of Vehlan into the floor, where the light converged—right beneath Idris's feet.

There was a *snap*—like the shattering of a mirror deep inside the earth.

The glyphs *screamed.*

Idris collapsed, his eyes rolling back, his breath coming in sharp, erratic gasps.

Kessa dropped to her knees beside him, searching his face. "Idris?"

His eyes fluttered. Recognition. Fear. And then stillness.

He was gone.

Not taken. Not screaming. Just... empty.

Aelira staggered back, her hands shaking. "He was awake in there. I could feel it. He was *aware*."

Calen caught her. "It's like drowning inside your own mind."

They stood in stunned silence.

Then the spire pulsed again—slow, deliberate.

The whisper came from everywhere at once.

"I showed you mercy. So you would understand me. Next time... I won't ask."

The glyphs went dark. The pulse slowed. The chamber grew still.

But it wasn't over.

Not yet.

Aelira looked at Idris's body. She didn't cry. Not this time.

Instead, she turned toward the spire, eyes burning with fire.

"It's learning from us," she said. "And we're *giving it everything it needs*."

Calen put a hand on her shoulder. "Then we starve it. We deny it its *narrative*. We fight not just with swords—but with truth."

Kessa stood, eyes still red. "Then we go back. We warn the city."

"No," Aelira said, staring into the darkness. "We do more than warn.

We *prepare for war*."

CHAPTER FORTY-FIVE: ALL MY VOICES

Zephyra was too quiet when they returned.

The sun shone as it always had. The wind stirred the banners above the walls. Children laughed in the distance.

But beneath it all, a hush had fallen.

Not peace. Not calm.

It was the stillness of a city listening to something only it could hear.

Aelira knew it within moments. The way people moved—too slow, too smooth. Their eyes didn't meet. They barely spoke.

At a corner stall, a merchant stood with her hands flat on the wood, breathing steadily but not blinking.

"I've never seen the city so quiet," Kessa said.

"It's not silence," Calen murmured. "It's submission."

They moved deeper into the city, toward the Council Hall. Everything looked intact—but the walls *felt* closer. The air *thicker*.

Whispers drifted between alleyways. Not voices. Not language. But *impulse*.

Calen rubbed at his temples, his Catalyst senses burning at the edges. "They're not being controlled," he said. "They're being *tuned*. Their worst thoughts are being pulled into focus."

"Like an echo chamber," Aelira said. "Of the soul."

Thale met them at the old gate. "Half the Council is gathering. But it's not to prepare. It's... submission. Surrender. They've convinced themselves there's no other path."

"To what?" Aelira asked.

"To survival. To quiet." He swallowed. "To the *Echo*."

They entered the chamber.

Once a place of fierce debate and vision, it now felt like a tomb. The council members sat in near-silence, some with blank stares, others mumbling to themselves.

One rose as Aelira entered.

"Princess," he said, smiling faintly. "It's good you've returned. We've been... discussing options."

She frowned. "You've been listening to it."

The man's smile widened. "It only speaks what we already fear."

And then—he turned his eyes toward her. Violet shimmered within.

Aelira's breath caught.

Calen moved.

He didn't hesitate.

His feet planted, fists clenched. And then he *shouted*—not with his voice, but with his *mind*.

NO.

YOU WILL NOT SPEAK THROUGH THEM.

WE ARE MORE THAN OUR FEARS.

I KNOW WHO I AM.

The air cracked.

A pulse of psychic pressure exploded from Calen, rippling through the chamber. Several councillors cried out. The shimmering in their eyes faded. One collapsed, gasping.

The taint recoiled.

The Echo screamed—a jagged cry not of sound, but of rage.

Aelira caught Calen as he staggered, blood trickling from his nose. His skin was clammy, his chest heaving.

"That was... too much," she whispered.

"I'll shout louder next time," he rasped.

The King entered then, eyes sharp despite his cane. "What just happened here?"

Aelira helped Calen steady himself. "The Echo's spreading through suggestion. Not force. It's *amplifying* what's already inside people. Doubt. Despair. Regret."

"It wants a city that bends before it rises," Calen added. "If we don't act, Zephyra will *offer* itself."

Thale looked to the others. "Then what do we do?"

Aelira turned toward the open chamber doors. Her jaw was set. "We do what it fears most."

She met the King's gaze. "We unite. And we speak. Not with lies, not with control. With truth. And will."

Calen wiped the blood from his nose. "I'll lead that charge. With every breath I've got left."

A whisper drifted through the still chamber, barely audible—but they all heard it.

"You shout now, Catalyst. But all flames flicker... before they die."

Aelira drew the Shard. It flared—bright, steady, defiant.

"Then you'll learn," she said softly, "how long fire can burn."

CHAPTER FORTY-SIX: THE FINAL PATTERN

The Council Hall was brighter the next morning—but the light felt wrong. It spilled in through high windows like melted gold, hazy and thin, casting long shadows that didn't quite match their sources.

Aelira stood at the centre of the room beside Calen and Thale, all eyes on the holomap projecting Zephyra's underground latticework.

What they saw was no accident of infrastructure.

Veins of red light pulsed like blood vessels from the Citadel ruins, branching out beneath the city in precise arcs and intersecting points—too deliberate to be coincidence.

Thale zoomed in on one junction. "This chamber—here. Beneath the observatory. We never built that."

Aelira nodded slowly. "It was there before Zephyra. Buried. Forgotten. Until the Echo remembered it."

Calen folded his arms, eyes narrowed. "It's a glyph. A summoning pattern drawn into the bedrock. And it's almost complete."

The King sat near the edge of the chamber, wrapped in furs against the chill that had settled over his bones since the Echo's first stirrings. His voice was soft but steady. "And if the Pattern finishes?"

Aelira turned. "It won't need a host anymore. It'll *become* one."

The silence that followed wasn't of disbelief. It was dread.

Thale's fingers hovered over the control pad. "A city-shaped vessel."

"No," Calen said quietly. "A *world-shaped thought.*"

The map flickered. Across it, pulsing red points now lit in sync—like a heart with too many chambers.

They made a plan.

The Core Nexus—directly beneath the ruins of the observatory—was the focal point. From there, they could disable the Pattern, if they reached it in time. But it was deep, shielded by rock, guarded by whispers.

"We can't bring an army," Aelira said. "Too many minds. Too much risk. A strike team only."

The King met her gaze. "And you'll lead them."

"I will."

She looked at Calen, who nodded without a word.

Later, she stood on the outer balcony alone, watching the city stir below her.

Zephyra looked peaceful. But she knew better.

Its people moved like those in dreams—murmuring half-memories, carrying burdens they could not name.

Calen stepped beside her.

"You should rest," he said.

"I can't."

He nodded. "Then let's just stand for a moment. Before it all begins."

They said nothing more. But their hands found each other.

And then—Aelira's breath caught.

The world *shifted*.

The air grew still.

And she was no longer on the balcony.

She stood in a vast underground chamber, the Core Nexus—but *wrong*. The stone was wet. Pulsing. Alive. The walls heaved like lungs, the floor rippling beneath her feet.

In the centre stood Calen.

Not bound. Not injured. But unmoving.

He stared at her, unblinking.

All around him—faces emerged from the walls. Idris. Ryven. Her mother. Her younger self.

They whispered: *"Let it in."*

The Shard was gone from her hand. Her voice wouldn't rise. Her will felt distant.

The Pattern pulsed in the floor. A circle etched in flesh and fire.

"Let it in."

The walls closed around her.

She choked.

And *woke*—gasping.

She was back on the balcony. Calen had caught her.

"What did you see?" he asked.

She shook her head. "The Pattern. Complete. The city alive, but not... human. A dream that couldn't wake."

She gripped the railing.

"We go tonight," she said. "Before the Pattern finishes. Before we forget who we are."

And far beneath them, in the cold pulse of the earth, the Echo stirred.

Not sleeping.

Only *waiting*.

CHAPTER FORTY-SEVEN: THE DESCENT

They gathered at twilight—no fanfare, no ceremony. Just the quiet discipline of people who knew the odds and stepped forward anyway.

The ruins of the old observatory loomed like a hollowed eye socket above them, its broken dome jutting against the sky. Beneath it, hidden by crumbled stone and centuries of overgrowth, lay a sealed shaft—recently uncovered and cleared by Thale's teams.

It dropped into the bones of the city like a spear.

Aelira stood at the edge, her sword at her side, the last rays of the sun brushing gold across her pauldrons. The air smelled of moss and ancient dust. Of secrets rising from below.

Calen joined her, strapping his gauntlet tight. "Still time to run."

She arched a brow. "You first."

He smiled, but it didn't reach his eyes. "Didn't think so."

Thale arrived behind them, adjusting a shoulder lamp, followed by two Echo-resistant Sentinels and a silent, hooded scout—Vey, the one touched by the Echo and returned... changed.

No one spoke as they began the descent.

The shaft spiralled downward, cut by hands long dead. The walls shifted from brick to stone to something older still—obsidian laced with silver veins, glowing faintly with unnatural light.

Ten meters. Twenty. Fifty.

With each turn, the air grew colder—yet the walls began to sweat.

"They're breathing," Calen muttered.

Aelira reached out and touched the surface. Warm. Almost alive. She drew back quickly.

They reached a landing—a half-ruined platform that opened onto a wide tunnel. Carvings spiralled along the ceiling: runes that didn't belong to any known script, but made the back of the mind itch.

"The glyph lines," Thale murmured, scanning the walls. "They converge here."

Aelira studied the floor—etched with faint channels like veins. "The Pattern finishes below. This is the throat of it."

They advanced slowly. The walls seemed to lean inward, narrowing as they moved. The glow brightened. And then—a sound.

Not heard. *Felt.*

A vibration in the chest, a whisper against the skull. No words—just presence.

Aelira's breath caught. "It's thinking."

"No," said Calen. "It's *listening.*"

They reached a threshold. A pair of stone doors stood ajar, thick and scarred. Beyond, darkness pulsed like a heartbeat.

"This is it," Aelira said. "The Nexus."

The air shimmered.

And then—her voice, but not hers, drifted from the dark beyond:

"Come closer, little sovereign. Come to where the truth was first buried. Come, and remember what you truly are."

Calen stepped up beside her. "Don't listen. It's trying to fracture your mind before you cross."

"I know." She steadied herself. "But I remember who I am."

"And I remember *you.*" Calen's voice softened, but his eyes held fire. "That's how we break it. Not with blades. With *truth.*"

Aelira turned, taking one last look behind. The narrow tunnel that had brought them here seemed suddenly distant, like a memory fading.

Then she faced forward.

"Let's make it bleed."

Together, they stepped into the dark.

CHAPTER FORTY-EIGHT: THE HEART OF THE NEXUS

The moment they stepped across the threshold, the world… changed.

It wasn't just the cold. It was a deep wrongness—like stepping into the echo of a dream you didn't remember having. The air thickened. Light bent unnaturally, casting shadows that moved of their own volition. The walls rippled, not physically, but *visually*, like something alive pulsing just beneath the surface.

Vey stopped first, her eyes losing focus. "We're inside its mind now. Or it's inside ours."

Calen stepped closer to Aelira, keeping his voice steady. "Stay with me. Don't trust what you see."

The Nexus chamber was a twisting contradiction—massive and confined, vast and claustrophobic. Its core loomed in the centre: a black-glass spire floating above a circular platform, its surface etched with glyphs in constant motion. Inside the spire swirled red-gold mist, pulsing to a rhythm that didn't match any heart, any world, any life.

Then—without warning—the world flickered.

Aelira gasped. Her father stood before her. Whole. Smiling. "You've come home, little one."

"No," she whispered, stumbling back. "No, you're gone."

The vision changed. She was in the palace gardens, no older than ten. Birds chirped, sunlight danced. But everything—too perfect. Too still. The sound of wings, frozen in the air.

She blinked hard—and the illusion fractured. Back in the chamber.

Beside her, Calen swayed, his hands clenching and unclenching. His old quarters. His mentor's voice. The scorn in Ryven's eyes. All of it pressing down, dragging at him.

Thale slammed a fist into the wall. "It's crawling inside our skulls."

"It's not real," Aelira said, her voice shaking. "It's *memory*—twisted into illusion."

"It's more than that," Vey said, her tone hushed. "It's *feeding*. Every doubt. Every ache. Every unspoken grief—it drinks from them."

Aelira turned to the spire. The red-gold mist brightened, as if it sensed her defiance.

And then—it *spoke*.

Voices—hers, Calen's, the King's, Ryven's, overlapping and wrong.

"You come seeking answers. But you are the answer. You seek to stop me, but I was born from you. From your pain. From the moment you chose fire over mercy. I am the wound beneath your crown."

"No," Aelira whispered, sword sliding from its sheath.

"You named yourself Catalyst," it hissed. *"But I made you. I made all of you. I am the Pattern. The pulse behind the stars. The breath that stirs when silence falls."*

Calen stepped forward, his gaze locked on the core. "You're not prophecy. You're the aftermath of cowardice. A shadow that grew fat on the past."

The spire cracked.

The chamber shuddered.

Images rained down—flashes of war, betrayal, love, loss. Calen's mother weeping. Aelira's bloodied hands. Ryven, triumphant over a broken city. And beneath it all, the sound of something *waiting*.

"Don't believe it!" Calen shouted over the roar. "Don't believe what it shows!"

Aelira trembled—but not from fear. "Then what do we believe in?"

Calen looked at her. *"Each other."*

She grabbed his hand—and the storm faltered.

Reality twisted again—but they held fast.

The mist inside the spire screamed.

The walls groaned. Stone split. The glyphs sparked wild, out of rhythm. Light pulsed erratically.

And then—the spire *bled*.

Not liquid, but memory. Tendrils of lost moments, regrets, phantom voices—all spilling into the air like smoke made of sorrow.

Aelira raised her sword. "You want truth?"

She slashed through the mist—and the Echo howled, recoiling.

"Here's mine: I'm not your vessel. I'm the flame that ends you."

A thunderous pulse rippled outward. The illusions broke. The Nexus peeled back—revealing its true shape: a cracked void surrounded by weeping statues of the ancient Starborn, each face contorted in agony.

But Aelira stood tall. Calen beside her. And for the first time since the Echo had awakened... it *recoiled*.

CHAPTER FORTY-NINE: WHAT BLEEDS, CAN DIE

The moment Aelira's blade cut through the swirling mist, the chamber *screamed.*

Not with voice—but with *existence.* The air fractured. The floor cracked open like glass under pressure. The black-glass spire twisted, shuddered, then ruptured in a bloom of raw memory and blazing crimson light.

The Echo had bled. Now it *fought back.*

Tendrils of shimmering red-gold lashed out, forming shapes—people, beasts, ghosts of war. They weren't real, but they carried *weight.* Aelira stumbled back as a phantom Ryven lunged at her, sword drawn, eyes burning with betrayal.

She parried on instinct, her blade colliding with illusion—but the force was real enough to send a shock through her arm.

Calen grabbed her shoulder. "It's manifesting now. No more tricks. This is its true form."

The centre of the chamber warped—rising into a mass of shifting light and shadow. From it emerged a being of liquid memory: faceless, featureless, ever-changing. Its form pulsed with fragments of everyone it had consumed—mothers, kings, rebels, children. Their voices wove into a single, thunderous cry.

*"You would end what cannot die."

"We would end what should never have lived,"* Calen replied, stepping forward, flame flaring from his palm.

The Echo surged.

It struck first.

A wave of crushing gravity rolled across the platform, slamming them to their knees. Calen gritted his teeth, hands glowing, pushing back with sheer will. Thale fired round after round at phantom shapes trying to flank them. Vey threw up a psychic barrier, sweat pouring from her brow.

The Echo coalesced into towering limbs of light and dark, lashing out. Each blow carved hollows in the air, tearing memories from stone. Statues cracked, murals bled, runes dissolved.

"It's unravelling the city's *past*," Vey choked. "This place is *built* from memory. If it dies, so does the Nexus."

"Then we end it before it ends *everything*," Aelira said, rising.

She looked the Echo dead in its seething heart. "You've taken everything from me. My mother. My peace. You almost took Calen."

The mist writhed violently.

"I'm taking *me* back."

She leapt.

Her blade cut through memory, through illusion, through pain. It struck the heart of the thing—and for a moment, the entire chamber flashed white.

The Echo convulsed. It screamed—its sound pure thought, drilling into skull and soul.

But Aelira stood firm. Calen was beside her in a heartbeat, his fire lancing through the exposed core. The mist peeled back, revealing a flickering seed of dark energy—twisting, pulsing, ancient.

"Now!" Vey cried. "That's its anchor!"

Calen hurled his flame. Aelira swung with all her strength.

The core cracked—

And the Echo shrieked, no longer mighty, no longer godlike—but *mortal*.

It began to fall apart. The shapes it had taken unravelled. The voices went silent, one by one. The chamber trembled with collapse.

But even as it died—it whispered.

"I was born of your silence. I will return... when you forget."—

Aelira stood over the crumbling remnants. "Then we'll never forget."

And with one final breath of defiance, the Echo dissolved into dust.

In the silence that followed, it wasn't victory that filled the chamber.

It was *clarity*.

The cost of it.

The weight.

The necessity.

And still ahead—the reckoning.

CHAPTER FIFTY: WHEN THE SILENCE BREAKS

The dust hadn't even settled.

Aelira knelt beside the broken edge of the platform, her breath sharp, the blade in her hand still humming from the final blow. Calen crouched next to her, eyes scanning the chamber that was no longer whole, no longer haunted—just fractured and fading.

The walls of the Nexus were crumbling, not from destruction, but from *release*.

Vey sat slumped against a pillar, blood trickling from her nose, her usually luminous gaze dulled to a flicker. Thale paced, his rifle slack in one hand, the other holding his comm unit to a dead line. No signals. No command. No outside world.

Only the hollow stillness where once there had been too many voices.

Calen brushed his fingers over Aelira's knuckles. She looked up, her eyes rimmed with exhaustion.

"We won," he said softly.

"Did we?" she asked.

He didn't answer immediately. Instead, he stood and offered his hand. She took it, and together they stepped through the fading shadows of the chamber, past broken illusions, splintered architecture, and the last flickering echoes of the Echo's domain.

The spiral stairs still held. The four of them climbed in silence.

Back on the surface, the world was... quieter.

The Nexus temple no longer stood tall. Its spires had collapsed inward, forming a skeletal crown against the skyline. People had gathered, survivors from the city, rebels and loyalists alike, drawn by the tremors, the light, the shift in the air.

No one knew what had happened—only that something had ended. Or begun.

Aelira stood before them, bruised and blood-streaked, her voice hoarse when she finally spoke.

"The Echo is gone."

Murmurs rippled like wind through leaves. No cheers. Not yet. The pain was too fresh.

She scanned the faces—people she had once ruled, once feared, once tried to save. Now, they looked at her not as a princess, but as someone *real*. Someone who had bled for them.

"It was not just a voice. It was every silence we allowed. Every wound we didn't speak of. Every fear we buried. That silence grew teeth."

She let the truth settle in.

"We end it by remembering. We rebuild, not just stone and steel, but trust."

There was no applause. But there was a murmur of assent. Heads bowed. Hands clasped.

Then Calen stepped beside her.

"We survived a ghost made from forgetting. So remember what matters. Each other."

A silence fell, not hollow like before—but *full.*

Later, as dusk fell and the city glowed in amber light, Aelira sat with her father.

The King had been quiet since his rescue, but now his hand found hers.

"I thought I had to pass on a kingdom," he murmured. "But what you've done... you gave them *hope.* That matters more than crowns."

She laid her head on his shoulder, just for a moment.

"And you gave me the strength to finish it."

He smiled faintly. "It's not finished yet."

And in the distance, past the last of the fading clouds, a new star rose.

A sign not of endings.

But of something *ready to begin.*

The next morning dawned gentle, golden. For the first time in weeks, no alarms rang, no battles brewed in the shadows. Just birdsong and rebuilding.

Aelira stood at the balcony of the royal quarters—what remained of them. The great hall had survived, its marble scorched but intact. Below, the city moved in quiet rhythm. People sweeping debris. Engineers stabilising shattered spires. Children playing in the dirt, as if to reclaim it.

The throne room had been converted into a gathering space. Not for orders, but for *dialogue*. Councillors and commoners spoke in equal measure. Old guards who once held rigid ranks now took tea with rebel scouts. There was unease, certainly—but there was *movement*.

Aelira entered slowly, flanked by Calen, Vey, and Thale. The room fell still.

She stood before the crowd, no longer wearing armour. Just a soft tunic and the crest of her house on a leather cord. No crown.

"My mother taught me that power isn't inherited—it's earned. And for too long, Zephyra clung to inheritance."

She gestured to the cracked stone floor. "Now, we earn it. Together."

A ripple of murmurs followed. Some sceptical. Others, relieved.

An elder woman in rebel green stood. "And what of the laws? Of those who profited from the silence?"

Aelira met her gaze. "Justice comes. But it will not be vengeance. It will be truth. We appoint new magistrates—balanced, from both sides."

There was a murmur of approval. Then a voice from the crowd:

"And you, Highness? Will you rule?"

She hesitated.

"I will lead... until you no longer need me. Until someone better rises. Someone chosen by all of you. My title is a bridge, not a throne."

Calen nodded beside her, proud. Vey watched with a quiet smile. Thale gave a soft, respectful grunt.

Later, in the quiet of the restored garden, Aelira and Calen sat beneath a tree older than the city.

"What now?" Calen asked.

She leaned against him.

"Now we build something that doesn't need saving every generation."

He kissed her temple. "With you, I'd build a hundred kingdoms."

She smiled faintly. "One will do. If it lasts."

And as the sun set over a city no longer fractured by fear, the future finally began to take root.

CHAPTER FIFTY-ONE:
WHISPERS OF THE STARBORN

The dreams returned first.

Calen had not dreamed in weeks—at least, not dreams that lingered. But now they came in fragments, slivers of memory dressed as prophecy. Stars spiralling through a glass dome. A woman of light, her face familiar and unknown, reaching toward him with silver-tipped fingers. A word barely whispered.

"Catalyst."

He sat up in the darkness, breath caught in his throat, the stone walls of the royal chambers cold around him. Aelira stirred beside him, sensing the shift, even in sleep.

"Another vision?" she murmured.

He nodded. "Different this time. Less... terror. More truth."

She leaned up, brushing hair from his eyes. "We should tell Vey."

By morning, the sky had turned grey-blue, soft with cloud cover. The war was over, the city mending—but unease clung like mist.

In the newly rebuilt council chamber, Calen sat with Vey, Thale, and Aelira. Before them stood a table littered with ancient fragments—metal plates etched in star-script, cracked circuits from the old ruins, and one strange, curved device that had pulsed to life the moment Calen entered the room.

"We found this," Vey said, tapping the strange arc. "Deep beneath the royal observatory. Locked behind three doors, sealed with a biometric cipher we couldn't breach."

"Until Calen walked past it," Thale added. "Then it just... opened."

Calen looked at it, wary. "I've never seen it before."

"But it's seen you," Vey said softly.

She activated the device. A soft hum rose, and a field of light shimmered in the air—a holographic display formed from nothing.

"Memory node," Vey explained. "Starborn tech. It stores ancestral memory. Blood-triggered."

Aelira reached for Calen's hand as a voice filled the room.

"Designation: Catalyst Prime. Lineage confirmed. Identity echo accepted. Initiating legacy recall."

The light shifted. Images danced—visions of planets wreathed in storms, colossal towers that moved like beasts, stars dying in slow spirals.

A face appeared: the woman from Calen's dreams. Pale-skinned, gold-eyed, a crest glowing at her throat.

"To my descendant… you carry the Flame. You are the last bridge between the Known and the Lost."

The projection flickered, then vanished.

Silence.

Thale finally said, "What in all hells does *that* mean?"

Vey folded her arms. "It means the Starborn left more than ruins. They left a *message*. A plan. And Calen is the key."

Calen stood slowly. "I never asked for this."

"But it's in you," Aelira said, firm but gentle. "And maybe the world needs more than peace—it needs memory. *Truth.*"

That night, Calen stood in the observatory ruins. The stars wheeled slowly overhead, their dance unhurried by mortal concerns.

The curved arc—now silent—rested in his hands.

"I don't know what you want from me," he whispered. "But I'll find out. Not because of fate. But because they trusted me. And I won't let them down."

A light blinked once on the device—acknowledgment? Approval?

He didn't know.

But somewhere, deep in the cosmos, something had begun to stir.

And it knew his name.

Later that night, the chamber was quiet, lit only by the fire burning low in the hearth. Calen sat at the edge of the bed, elbows on his knees, staring at the embers as if they could give him answers.

Aelira entered quietly, her footsteps soft against the stone floor. She crossed the room and placed her hand gently on his shoulder.

"You're carrying the weight of stars again," she said, kneeling before him.

He let out a slow breath. "What if I'm not enough? What if this legacy… this 'Catalyst Prime'—what if it's more than I can handle?"

Her hand found his. She brought it to her chest, pressing it over her heart. "You're not alone in this.

You never have been. Whatever the stars ask of you, I'll be there beside you."

He looked into her eyes—clear, unwavering. "You believe I can do this?"

"With all of me," she said. "Not because some ancient voice says so. But because I've seen who you are. I've fought beside you, bled with you, loved you. And I know what you're made of."

Her words settled into him like balm to a wound. The doubt didn't vanish entirely, but it was no longer in command.

He leaned forward, resting his forehead against hers. "Thank you," he whispered.

She smiled softly. "You can thank me properly in the morning."

But he didn't wait until then.

What followed was a quiet storm of closeness and longing, of lips that spoke without words and touches that promised everything. Not hurried. Not desperate. But *true*. A reaffirmation of their bond, forged not only in war, but in quiet strength and abiding love.

And when the dawn broke, Calen no longer looked like a man afraid of destiny.

He looked like someone ready to walk toward it.

CHAPTER FIFTY-TWO: LEGACY AWAKENED

The morning air was crisp with a soft veil of mist clinging to the palace gardens. Dew sparkled on the petals of sleeping blooms, and the scent of wet stone carried on the breeze. Calen stood alone at the edge of the fountain, hands clasped behind his back, watching the ripples dance across the water.

The night's embrace still lingered in his skin, the warmth of Aelira's belief grounding him. Yet the questions remained, persistent as ever.

He turned as footsteps approached. Aelira, wrapped in a deep blue cloak, her silver hair cascading over her shoulder, moved to stand beside him.

"Did the stars answer you?" she asked gently.

He offered a wry smile. "Not in the way I hoped. But maybe I'm finally ready to ask the right questions."

She touched his arm. "Then we'll ask them together."

Moments later, Vey joined them, carrying a datapad etched with shimmering Starborn glyphs. Her expression was serious.

"The device you activated last night—it didn't just show a vision," she said. "It uploaded coordinates.

Five of them. Each one linked to ancient Starborn outposts scattered across the world."

Calen blinked. "And you think they're still active?"

"Possibly. Or at least intact enough to contain answers. Maybe weapons. Maybe history. Whatever they are, they were hidden from everyone—until now."

Aelira peered over Vey's shoulder, frowning. "Shattered Reach is first? That's not exactly a welcoming start. It's remote. Untamed."

Thale arrived, sword belted at his hip, brows furrowed. "Echo Council wants to convene this afternoon. Word's spread about the projection. The nobles are getting restless. They want to know if we've just traded one war for another."

Calen sighed. "Then we give them something to believe in. Tell them the truth—some of it."

"Which truth?" Thale asked. "That our Catalyst is bonded to ancient alien memory? That our future may lie in forgotten ruins across the continent?"

Calen smiled faintly. "No. We tell them what they need to hear. That we're not done rebuilding. That the peace is real, but fragile. And that we intend to *strengthen* it."

"And the rest?"

"We keep for ourselves. Until we know more."

Aelira nodded. "We leave tonight. Under cover of dark. First coordinates lead to the Shattered Reach. It's not far—but it's wild."

"Then we take only who we trust."

Vey handed him the datapad. "And we move quickly. Because if this legacy truly awakened, it didn't just awaken for you."

Calen looked toward the horizon, where the mist gave way to faint sunlight. His voice was quiet, but resolute.

"They'll come looking."

"And we'll be ready," Aelira whispered, taking his hand.

She squeezed gently, and he met her gaze with a steadiness he hadn't known even a day ago. The fire had returned to his eyes—not born of anger or fear, but of purpose.

Beneath them, the earth hummed faintly—whether memory or omen, none could say.

But the stars were watching.

CHAPTER FIFTY-THREE: THE SHATTERED REACH

Night fell fast in the borderlands. The moon, fractured into slivers by passing cloud, lent only the faintest glow to the path. They moved in silence through the forest's edge, shadows among shadows, each step taking them farther from the comforts of Virelia and deeper into the wilder, ungoverned places of the world.

Calen led the way, datapad strapped to his belt and sword on his hip. Aelira flanked him, her cloak hooded, eyes constantly scanning the trees. Vey moved at their rear, navigating by ancient glyphs projected in quiet bursts of light. Thale, grim and watchful, took the high ground whenever he could, covering their approach like a ghost.

The Shattered Reach earned its name well. Once a fertile valley, it had been torn apart by seismic upheaval centuries ago—jagged ravines now crisscrossed the land like old scars. Massive shards of crystalline rock jutted from the soil, humming with dormant energy that made the air feel thick with static.

They stopped at the edge of a narrow gorge, the bridge long since crumbled.

"We're close," Vey murmured, eyes on the datapad. "Within five hundred metres."

Calen peered down into the ravine. The far side shimmered faintly with a bluish glow.

"There's power down there."

"Old power," Aelira said, her voice low. "It tastes like... memory."

"Or a trap," Thale added. "These places don't stay untouched for this long without reason."

Calen crouched, brushing his hand along the stone. It pulsed faintly beneath his palm.

"It knows I'm here," he whispered.

Aelira placed a hand on his shoulder. "Then make it remember who you are."

They descended into the gorge cautiously, boots scraping over loose rock. The deeper they went, the stronger the sensation became—like walking into a storm not yet broken. Finally, they reached a clearing. In its centre rose a massive arch of fractured crystal, half-buried and slanted, its surface covered in ancient Starborn glyphs.

The moment Calen stepped near, the arch came alive.

A pulse of blue light rippled through the clearing. The symbols lit up one by one, the ground beneath their feet vibrating. A low, harmonic hum spread outward, resonating with the very bones of the land.

"Welcome... Starborn," a voice echoed—metallic, ancient, and not entirely real.

Everyone froze.

"What was that?" Thale hissed, drawing his sword.

Calen's eyes were wide. "It spoke... to me."

A shimmering veil unfolded beneath the arch. A gateway, or perhaps a recording—Calen couldn't tell. Within it danced flickering shapes: a city among the stars, a figure cloaked in energy, and a dying sun. It wasn't just a message—it was an invitation.

Vey's voice broke the silence. "I think it wants you to step through."

"Alone?" Aelira asked sharply.

The veil shimmered again, and this time, a second pulse rolled through the arch—gentler. Two threads of light reached outward, wrapping around both Calen and Aelira.

"No," Calen said, breathless. "It knows her too."

Without waiting, they stepped forward together.

The world dissolved.

For a heartbeat, there was only light.

CHAPTER FIFTY-FOUR: THE VEILED MEMORY

Light surrounded them—fluid, warm, and without edge. Calen felt weightless, drifting in a sea of stars. There was no sound, no breath, no body. Only a presence—a memory pressing against the edges of his mind like a whisper waiting to be heard.

Then the world snapped into focus.

They stood together on a vast platform of silver and glass, suspended in the middle of a sky untouched by sun or moon. Above them, stars wheeled slowly in a perfect spiral. Below, there was nothing—no land, no sea, only the infinite dark. The air vibrated with energy, like standing at the heart of a storm held in pause.

Aelira clutched Calen's hand tightly. "Where are we?"

"Not a place," he said quietly, "a memory."

As if summoned by his words, images bloomed into being—flickers of moments from a distant age. Starborn cities floating in orbit above lush blue worlds. Towers that shimmered with living metal. People in robes of white and gold, their faces noble, their eyes bearing the light of understanding. Great spires channelling cosmic energy into radiant fields that sustained entire continents.

Then—

Flame.

The stars were dying. One by one, they collapsed into themselves, pulled into a void not of nature, but of intent. A presence emerged in the vision—dark, formless, vast. Not a creature, but a force. The *Unmaking*. Its touch consumed suns, devoured memory, and left behind silence.

Aelira gasped. "That's the thing that's coming."

The memory fractured, reformed. Calen stood alone in a chamber of stone and fire. Before him, a Starborn elder—tall, cloaked in silver light—pressed a glowing orb into his hands.

"You are the Catalyst," the figure intoned. "The bridge between what was and what must be. The heart must burn for the world to endure."

The vision shifted again. This time, Calen saw his own face reflected in the obsidian surface of the orb. But it was not *his* face—it was the same, yet older, worn, eyes fierce with resolve. He looked... like a leader. One shaped by loss, tempered by sacrifice.

Around the orb, ruins emerged. Twisted pylons, charred metal, the remnants of something once magnificent. A broken place where no stars shone.

A voice whispered: "Return to the place where the stars were silenced. There lies the truth of what you are."

Calen turned in the vision and saw the outline of a constellation etched into a stone map—one that looked eerily familiar. He tried to reach for it.

The world shuddered.

The memory began to unravel, like mist caught in wind.

"Wait—" Calen stepped forward.

But the light collapsed inward, pulling them from the memory.

Calen and Aelira stumbled back into the gorge, gasping. The veil vanished. The arch was dim again. The air felt heavy, the silence charged.

Calen dropped to his knees, still dazed. "I saw it. A place of ruin... under a dead sky. I think I know where it is."

Aelira knelt beside him, placing her hand on his chest. "Then that's where we go."

He nodded, slowly regaining his breath. "We're not just following a trail anymore."

"We're walking into the past," she said, "to save the future."

Above them, the stars had begun to shift.

The night air still clung to them, cool and sharp, as Calen and Aelira made their way back to camp. The rest of the company had grown silent under the weight of uncertainty, but the moment Calen emerged from the canyon, a shift passed through the group like wind over tall grass.

He didn't need to speak. They could see it in his eyes—something had changed.

Neran stepped forward. "You found something."

Calen gave a small nod. "A memory... a warning. And a destination."

He turned to the gathered group, voice steady. "There's a place—somewhere far from here. A ruin where the stars were once silenced. The memory showed it to me. I believe it holds the truth of what I am, and what the Starborn were trying to stop."

A murmur passed through the soldiers and scholars alike. Unspoken fear lingered beneath the surface.

Aelira stepped beside him. "We leave at dawn."

They broke camp with quiet urgency, moving quickly through the last of the gorge and into the windswept valley beyond. By midday, the terrain changed again—jagged cliffs gave way to salt-stained flats where ancient bones of leviathans lay half-buried in the dust.

Calen rode ahead, scanning the horizon. The constellation etched in the stone map from the memory flickered through his mind again. He could see its shape—just barely—aligned with the peaks in the distance.

They were heading in the right direction.

As the sun lowered, Aelira rode up beside him. "You've been quiet."

He exhaled slowly. "It's strange... I feel like I've known this path before. Like my feet remember where to step, even when my mind hesitates."

"That's what legacy is," she said, her voice soft. "It's not just memory—it's instinct. Buried deep."

They camped near the mouth of a ravine that night. Fires crackled low. Wind whispered over stone.

Calen found himself staring at the stars, tracing the pattern from the vision.

"Do you think they meant for you to see all of this?" Aelira asked, settling beside him.

"I don't know," he replied. "But if they did... it means they believed I could do something about it."

"And they were right," she said simply. "You're not alone in this, Calen."

He looked at her then—really looked—and the weight on his shoulders seemed lighter. He took her hand and gave it a gentle squeeze.

Tomorrow, they would reach the threshold of the forgotten. But tonight, they had each other.

CHAPTER FIFTY-SIX: THE RUINS OF SILENCE

The sky had taken on a strange hue—an ashen twilight that neither deepened nor faded. The land they crossed was a scar, weathered and vast, the air tinged with the scent of old ash and ancient metal. The peaks from Calen's vision rose ahead, jagged as teeth, and beyond them, nestled in a crater, lay the ruins.

They arrived at dusk.

The remnants of a once-mighty structure stretched across the valley floor, fractured spires and broken conduits etched with Starborn markings. But there was no life. No hum of energy. No stars above. Even the sky itself felt... still.

"This is it," Calen whispered. "The place where the stars were silenced."

The wind howled low across the broken stone. Aelira stepped forward, fingers brushing a column half-buried in dust. Symbols flared briefly beneath her touch—Starborn script, faded and incomplete.

Neran and the others followed, weapons drawn, though there was no immediate threat. Only silence.

"This place is dead," said one of the soldiers.

"No," Calen said quietly, kneeling beside an exposed ring of metal. "It's sleeping."

He touched the symbol at its centre.

Pain lanced through his mind.

A memory erupted: a Starborn vessel screaming into orbit. A warning beacon blaring across systems. A name—*Ryven*—and the word *traitor*.

He staggered back.

"Calen!" Aelira caught him.

He gritted his teeth. "I saw it... Ryven destroyed this place. He betrayed the Starborn. This was a last stand."

Neran stepped closer. "Then we're standing in a tomb."

"No," Calen said. "We're standing at the threshold of the truth. And Ryven didn't just destroy this—he *erased* it from memory. That's why the stars here are gone. He used the Echo's power to rip this place from the minds of the galaxy."

Aelira's voice trembled. "Then what brought it back?"

"You did," Calen said, looking at her. "Your presence... your bond to me. It woke something. The Echo couldn't hold it once we remembered."

They moved deeper into the ruins, descending into what once had been a sanctuary. Pillars bent inward like reaching fingers. A central chamber waited below, lined with dark stone.

In the centre sat a dais, and on it... a sphere.

The Heart of the Nexus.

Calen stepped forward. The sphere pulsed faintly, responding to his presence.

"This is what it was all for," he murmured. "This... is our legacy."

CHAPTER FIFTY-SEVEN: THE MEMORY RECLAIMED

The chamber was cloaked in half-light. Dust hung thick in the air, disturbed only by the faint pulse of the Nexus Heart. Its glow was rhythmic—like breath. Calen felt it resonate beneath his ribs, matching the beat of his own heart.

He reached out slowly. The sphere stirred to life, shedding shadows like old skin. Symbols spiralled across its surface—glyphs older than language.

As his fingers brushed it, light flared.

The chamber vanished.

Calen stood suspended in memory, surrounded by fragments of the past. A Starborn council, voices raised in alarm. Ryven—younger, proud, eyes like burning coals—standing at the centre. He argued not for conquest, but for dominance. "The Catalyst is wasted on guardianship. We could reshape the void itself."

Others shouted him down.

Then came fire. Betrayal. Ryven unleashing the Echo, warping memory, devouring worlds. One by one, the Starborn fell, and their legacy was entombed in silence.

Calen collapsed to his knees, breath stolen by the enormity of it.

The vision shifted.

Now he stood before the same dais, long ago, as another man—tall, regal, bearing the Catalyst's sigil burned into his palm. His name lost, but his purpose clear.

He sealed the Heart away, uttering a final vow:

"If the darkness rises again, let the flame be reborn. Let memory find its bearer. Let the Catalyst awaken."

Calen gasped.

The memory broke.

He was back, trembling. Aelira knelt beside him, gripping his shoulders. "What did you see?"

"Everything." His voice was hoarse. "Ryven didn't just betray the Starborn—he *unmade* them. He used the Echo to destroy their legacy. But one of them… one of them knew. He saved this, sealed it for me."

Neran stepped closer. "And now?"

Calen looked at the Heart. "Now it's awake."

The sphere rose, drifting toward him. It pulsed brighter—faster—until it hovered before his chest. A thread of light reached out, touching the place over his heart.

There was no pain, only warmth. It sank into him.

The Heart became one with the Catalyst.

Calen staggered but did not fall.

The silence of the chamber shattered. The ground shook. Outside, a rumble tore through the valley.

The Echo had felt it.

"It knows," Calen whispered. "It knows I remember."

They ran.

CHAPTER FIFTY-EIGHT: THE UNSEEN HAND

The ground still trembled beneath their boots as they emerged from the sanctuary, the ruins alive with an energy that hadn't stirred in centuries. The stars above flickered back into being—dim at first, like a memory returning, then sharp and cold.

"What now?" Neran asked, scanning the dark ridges.

"We move," Calen said. His voice had changed—deeper, steadier. The Heart pulsed faintly beneath his shirt, a second heartbeat now always with him. "We don't give Ryven time to strike."

Aelira moved to his side. "We need to reach your father. If the Echo knows, Ryven won't wait for the Council to convene."

A shiver crawled down her spine, and Calen felt it too. Not fear—forewarning.

They made haste down the slope, shadows chasing their steps. But even as they moved, Calen's thoughts flickered to the feeling he couldn't shake they were being watched.

By dawn, they reached the edge of the crystalline fields. Once vibrant, they now hummed with discordant energy.

Then—

A whisper.

No voice. No source.

Just an echo in Calen's mind.

"Your path ends here, Catalyst."

He spun. No one there.

But Neran stumbled, clutching his head.

"They're in my mind," he gasped. "It's him—Ryven—he's reaching through the Echo."

Calen narrowed his eyes. He focused, clenched his jaw, and pushed outward with his thoughts—not speaking, but shouting inside.

You have no hold over us.

The presence wavered.

You remember, yes... but remembering is not understanding. You walk paths others carved in fear. I walk in truth.

Calen ground his teeth. "We have to block him out."

Aelira placed her hand on his. "Then let's remind him we're not afraid."

Calen raised his hand, palm out. The Heart pulsed through his skin—and a flare of light burst across the field. The dissonant energy shattered like glass, and the air cleared.

Silence.

But it would not last.

Behind them, in the ruins, something stirred.

A sentinel of Ryven's making—shadow-forged and etched with false Starborn sigils—stepped into the waking world.

Its eyes burned like coals.

Calen turned to face it, drawing the flame from within. "Let's see how long his puppet lasts."

CHAPTER FIFTY-NINE: THE SHADOW FORGED

The sentinel towered over them—eight feet of shadow-wrought alloy, its surface shimmering with a dark iridescence. Veins of crimson pulsed along its limbs like molten blood. The false Starborn sigils etched into its plating twisted as if alive, warping ancient meaning into mockery.

"Calen..." Aelira's voice was low but steady. "This isn't like the others."

"I know."

It moved—fast. A blur of black and red crashing forward, the impact of its footfall cracking the crystalline earth. Neran dove aside just in time. The sentinel's blade arm came down in a hiss of searing energy.

Calen threw up a shield, the Heart flaring with golden flame. The blade slammed into the barrier, sending out a thunderclap that knocked everyone back.

The force rattled his bones. "It's feeding off the Echo," he gasped. "It's *made* of it."

They regrouped quickly.

Aelira drew her Starsteel daggers, eyes burning with fury. "Then we starve it."

She charged, blades slicing across the sentinel's leg. Sparks flew, but the creature didn't falter. It pivoted with uncanny grace, backhanding her with a sweep of its massive arm. She hit the ground hard, breath driven from her lungs.

Calen roared.

Power surged.

The air around him shimmered with heat as the Heart ignited. Flame poured from his hands—not wild or uncontrolled, but channelled, precise. He leapt, slamming a wave of pure energy into the sentinel's chest.

It staggered, screeching—metal warped under the force. But even wounded, it raised its other arm, revealing a cluster of echo-crystals embedded in the forearm.

They lit up.

A sonic blast exploded outward. Calen was thrown backward, the flame around him momentarily extinguished.

Neran fired his arc-bow—three shots in succession. One embedded in the sentinel's neck. Another in the knee joint. The third missed.

Aelira was already up, sprinting forward again.

"Calen, *now!*" she shouted.

He forced himself upright. The Heart pulsed in time with his heartbeat—faster now, frantic.

He closed his eyes, centred himself, and shouted—not aloud, but into the Echo itself.

This is not your vessel. I sever your hold.

The creature hesitated—then shrieked as golden flame erupted from within.

The sigils unravelled.

With a final burst of light, the sentinel exploded into black shards that disintegrated before they hit the ground.

Silence returned.

Aelira leaned on him, blood at her temple, breath ragged. "That... was new."

Calen managed a grin. "We're just getting started."

CHAPTER SIXTY: THE EYE OF THE STORM

They camped in the hollow of a broken hill, the remnants of the sentinel still smouldering in the distance. The sky above them churned with slate clouds, silent but heavy, as though the heavens themselves were holding their breath.

Aelira sat beside Calen, legs pulled close, her eyes on the sky. Her temple was wrapped in a strip of gauze Neran had torn from his cloak, and her dark hair hung loose around her face.

"I thought we were ready," she murmured.

"We *were*," Calen replied, gently placing a hand over hers. "But Ryven's always three moves ahead. That's what makes him dangerous."

She looked at him then—not as the Catalyst, not as the one bearing the Heart, but as *Calen*. The man who stood beside her when the stars fell, who held her hand when silence filled the world.

"And yet... he didn't win," she said softly.

"No," Calen said. "But he *learned* something. So did we."

Neran stoked the fire a few feet away, his eyes never far from the horizon. "He sent that creature not to kill—but to *test*."

Calen nodded. "He wanted to see how strong the bond is. Between the Heart. Between us."

Aelira exhaled through her nose. "He saw enough."

"No," Calen said, leaning closer, his voice low. "He only saw the surface."

She turned to him, surprised by the sudden fire behind his eyes.

"The legacy awakened something in me. But you— you've *always* been my centre. Ryven thinks he can break me. But he doesn't understand what holds me together."

Aelira brushed her fingers against his jaw. "Then let's make him understand."

They sat in silence for a while, the storm above rumbling distantly.

"What's our next move?" Neran asked.

"We go to Zephyra," Calen said. "To the Citadel. My father needs to know what we've seen. And the Echo Council must be warned."

"And if the Council is already compromised?" Aelira asked.

Calen stared into the flames. "Then we flush the corruption out. We drag it into the light."

Neran nodded slowly. "We'll need allies."

"And answers," Aelira added.

"Then let's get both," Calen said. "Before Ryven makes his next move."

The storm above them finally cracked with thunder—but the fire at their feet burned steady.

CHAPTER SIXTY-ONE: ASH AND ECHO

The approach to Zephyra was nothing like Calen remembered.

Once a soaring beacon of hope nestled among the peaks, the city now crouched beneath a veil of smoke. Great banners bearing the sigil of the crown still fluttered from the spires, but the streets below were hushed. Too hushed.

They entered through the eastern gate beneath the cover of dawn, their small party moving like whispers through a city that seemed to hold its breath.

Aelira walked close beside Calen, her hand lightly brushing his as they scanned the buildings. "Where is everyone?" she whispered.

Neran pointed toward the market square. "Look."

Scorched ground. Blackened stone. A once-busy plaza now silent and grey.

"The Echo's been here," Calen said grimly.

"Not just the Echo," Aelira added. "This feels... orchestrated."

A sharp cry echoed from the far end of the square. They ducked into shadow as a figure emerged—

cloaked in deep violet, etched with silver runes. Echo-marked.

It wasn't alone. Two more followed, dragging a bound man between them.

"That's—" Calen started, then stopped. Recognition hit. "Commander Varris. One of my father's top guards."

They watched as the Echo agents forced him to his knees, speaking words too quiet to hear. But the meaning became clear when one drew a blade.

Calen moved.

There was no time for planning.

He flared into the open with a wave of force that sent one of the cloaked figures tumbling. Neran's bow thrummed behind him, striking the other in the shoulder.

Aelira sprinted to Varris, slicing his bonds in a blur.

The third figure—the leader—raised a hand, and a ripple of distortion swept toward them.

Calen braced, letting the Heart absorb it, reflecting the wave back in a blast of golden flame. The figure screamed as the magic backfired, tearing the mask from their face.

It was a woman. Young. Her eyes burned with Echo.

She collapsed into ash.

Silence returned.

Varris staggered to his feet, clutching Aelira's arm. "You—he told me you were dead."

"Reports of our demise," Aelira said, "are greatly exaggerated."

Calen stepped forward. "What happened here?"

"They took control fast. Nobles fell in line. The Echo Council shut down communications. Your father is missing."

"Missing?" Calen asked.

"Since the bombing of the High Chamber."

A chill ran through them all.

Calen looked to the horizon. "Then we've come back not to warn Zephyra…"

"…but to save it," Aelira finished.

CHAPTER SIXTY-TWO: CITADEL IN SHADOW

The outer gates of the Citadel loomed ahead, wreathed in mist and watched by statues older than the city itself. Once a place of honour and strategy, the heart of the Crown's strength, now it stood dim and hushed—like a breath held too long.

Calen and Aelira moved with purpose, flanked by Neran and the wounded Commander Varris. Varris, though weak, guided them through lesser-known tunnels carved for escape centuries ago.

"These passageways haven't been used in decades," he muttered. "Most think they're sealed."

"Let's keep it that way," Neran said, watching the rear.

They emerged in a side corridor near the Hall of Crowns. Smoke lingered in the air, and old blood marked the floor. The banners were still intact, but the silence screamed.

"The throne room is this way," Varris whispered.

They crept through marbled corridors until the main doors loomed ahead—partially ajar. Two Echo-marked guards flanked the entry.

Calen exchanged a glance with Aelira, then nodded.

It took mere seconds. Aelira blinked forward in a shimmer of light, her blade sweeping low. Neran's arrow dropped the second guard before his shout left his throat. Calen shoved the doors open.

Inside, the throne stood empty.

But not unguarded.

A group of nobles in silver-trimmed robes stood in half-circle before it—Echo Councillors. Eyes glowing. Mouths silent.

At their centre stood **Ryven**.

Or what looked like him.

His body was clad in blackened armour etched with spiralling runes. His hair hung loose, and the mark of the Echo pulsed on his brow—but the edges of his face seemed... unfinished. Like smoke given shape. Like he wasn't entirely *here*.

"A puppet," Aelira said.

Calen stepped forward. "Where's my father?"

The Ryven-puppet smiled. "Closer than you think. And further than you'll ever reach."

The Councillors began to chant.

The very walls trembled.

Runes flared across the floor—binding glyphs forming a trap.

"Back!" Neran shouted.

But Calen stood firm. "No. I came to *end* this."

He raised his hand—and the Heart pulsed.

The runes sputtered. Faltered. Then exploded outward, throwing the Councillors to the floor.

Ryven's puppet hissed and lunged—only for Aelira to intercept, her blade cleaving through the illusion.

Smoke. Nothing more.

But Calen's expression hardened.

"He's in the Spire," he said. "I can *feel* him."

"And he knows you're coming," Aelira replied.

"Good," Calen said. "Let him prepare."

CHAPTER SIXTY-THREE: THE HOLLOW CROWN

The lift that rose through the Spire groaned under ancient weight. Crafted centuries ago to carry kings and their closest to the crown's peak, it now bore a different kind of royalty—one forged not in lineage but in fire.

Calen stood with his hand on the edge, staring upward through the narrow shaft as gears ground and chains whispered.

Aelira was silent beside him, her gaze fixed on the rising walls. Every floor they passed bore signs of the struggle—shattered windows, flickering torches, the broken remnants of power.

Neran and Varris stood behind, weapons drawn, eyes sharp.

"This is where it began," Calen said softly. "My visions... the dreams. They always end here."

"Then maybe it's time they changed," Aelira whispered.

The lift stopped with a shudder.

They stepped into the upper chamber, the pinnacle of the Spire.

The throne was gone.

In its place stood a twisted sculpture of black metal, shaped like a crown but large enough to swallow a man whole. It pulsed with Echo energy, drawing in the shadows like breath.

And bound in chains of aether and steel, suspended within the sculpture's frame, was **King Vaelori**.

His eyes fluttered open at their approach. Weak. But alive.

"Aelira... Calen..."

A voice echoed behind them.

"You found him faster than I expected."

Ryven.

The real Ryven.

No smoke. No puppet. Only the man—reborn in the storm.

He stepped from the far shadows, clad in the same armour Calen had seen in his dreams. But now, the runes glowed crimson. His presence rippled across the chamber like heat.

"You were never supposed to reach this far," he said. "But I underestimated you both."

Calen took a step forward. "Let him go."

"Of course," Ryven smiled. "As soon as you take his place."

Aelira raised her blade. "Try me."

Ryven lifted his hand—and the crown pulsed, sending out a wave of force that knocked them all to their knees.

Only Calen stood.

The Heart flared.

Ryven's smile faded.

"So… the Catalyst finally awakens."

Calen's voice rang clear. "I'm not here to take the crown, Ryven. I'm here to destroy it."

He hurled his will into the Heart—and the crown screamed.

Cracks formed. Chains snapped.

Vaelori fell.

Aelira caught him. Neran moved to guard.

Ryven stepped forward, his voice cold. "Then you've chosen war."

Calen met his gaze. "No. I've chosen *freedom*."

CHAPTER SIXTY-FOUR: BLOOD OF THE STORM

Lightning cracked outside the shattered windows of the Spire, illuminating the swirling clouds above Zephyra. The Heart pulsed in Calen's chest, answering Ryven's challenge with a flare of energy that shook the entire tower.

The false crown fractured behind him, its runes bleeding light, but Ryven advanced unfazed—an obsidian blade manifesting in his hand, wicked and alive with Echo energy.

"You've defied fate long enough," Ryven said, his voice low and calm. "You think love and legacy will save you? You think *hope* is stronger than the storm?"

Calen drew his blade. "No. I think it *creates* the storm."

They collided like titans. Echo against Catalyst.

Each blow sent shockwaves through the chamber. Calen's blade sang with Heart-forged light, parrying Ryven's strikes that reeked of corrupted magic. Aelira moved to join, but the Heart flared—a barrier flung her and the others back.

"No," Calen gasped. "He's mine."

Ryven snarled. "Then die alone."

Their blades locked, sparks raining.

Below, the city trembled. The corrupted Crown had acted as a beacon—and now remnants of the Echo horde surged toward the Spire. Neran shouted orders as defenders rallied. Aelira cradled her father, whispering life into his battered spirit.

But above, gods clashed.

Ryven lashed out with tendrils of shadow, but Calen severed them with focused strikes, the Heart pulsing stronger with every truth he remembered—his mother's sacrifice, his friends' loyalty, Aelira's unwavering belief.

"I *am* the storm," Calen said. "And I will not be controlled."

He surged forward, driving Ryven back, strike after punishing strike until the corrupted blade shattered.

Ryven staggered.

"No," he whispered. "You were *mine* to shape."

"You were never my fate," Calen said.

And with one final thrust, he drove his blade into Ryven's chest.

The runes flickered.

Ryven's body convulsed, the Echo mark on his brow cracking like glass—

—and then, silence.

The storm above began to break.

The Heart dimmed.

Calen collapsed to one knee, panting.

Aelira rushed to his side, wrapping her arms around him as Neran and Varris secured the chamber.

"It's done," she whispered.

Calen looked to the sky. "Not yet. But it's ending."

CHAPTER SIXTY-FIVE: WHAT REMAINS

The sky over Zephyra was bruised with ash and fading storm light. The once-raging clouds had scattered like retreating armies, and a soft rain fell— not the thunderous wrath of before, but cleansing. Cool. Almost gentle.

Calen stood atop the Spire, overlooking the fractured city.

Below, the people of Zephyra emerged from hiding. Fires were being smothered. Cries of mourning blended with songs of survival. The palace bells, long silenced, rang again—not in fear, but as a call to gather.

He felt the Heart flicker faintly in his chest. Diminished, but still present. Changed.

Aelira stepped beside him, her arm threading through his. She had barely left his side since the battle.

"It's quiet," she said.

He nodded. "For now."

Behind them, King Vaelori rested in a recovery ward, stable but silent. The healers spoke of slow progress. Neran and Varris organized aid and patrols. The rebellion, without Ryven's iron grip, had fractured into confusion.

But they knew it wasn't over.

"Parts of the city still burn," Calen said. "And the Council… the real ones… we haven't found them all."

Aelira turned to him. "You said this wasn't about a throne."

"It still isn't."

"Then what will you do?"

He took a breath, eyes locked on the horizon.

"We rebuild. We tell the truth. We break the old order and let the people choose what rises in its place."

She smiled. "Then let's do it together."

He looked at her—truly looked—and nodded. "Always."

Behind them, the Heart of the Nexus pulsed once more, its energy no longer consuming, but calm. Listening.

Below, a city rose from its knees.

The storm had passed.

EPILOGUE: DAWN BEYOND THE STORM

Months had passed.

Zephyra had changed.

Gone were the banners of the old regime. In their place flew a new crest—wings outstretched above a rising sun, a symbol not of royalty, but of rebirth.

The Echo Council had been dismantled. Their strongholds emptied, their secrets exposed. The people had come together, not under a single ruler, but a provisional assembly—formed by those who had suffered, fought, and endured. From artisans to engineers, farmers to philosophers, voices long silenced now shaped the future.

Calen sat beneath the crystalline arch of the rebuilt Star Chamber. He wore no crown. No armour. Just the robes of a traveller, pale grey with threads of aether stitched along the hem.

He was no longer Catalyst of war—but of something more enduring.

Aelira entered quietly, a bundle of parchments in her arms. Her eyes met his, warm as morning light. She had taken her place as a leader among equals—both loved and respected, not because of birthright, but because of the strength she had shown when the world fell apart.

"They agreed to the charter," she said. "Unanimously. The people will vote this spring."

Calen exhaled with relief. "Then we've done it."

She smiled, setting the parchments down and coming to stand beside him. "Not done. *Begun*."

Outside, children played in the streets where once soldiers had marched. The Heart's pulse had faded into legend, resting beneath the city, no longer a weapon—but a memory.

Aelira leaned her head against his shoulder. "Do you ever wonder what it would have been like—if we'd never crashed on that world?"

Calen chuckled. "No. Because we'd never have found each other."

She looked up at him. "And now?"

"Now," he said, taking her hand, "we build the kind of world we never thought we'd see. One worthy of the love we found in its ruins."

She leaned in, brushing her lips to his.

Beyond the Star Chamber, Zephyra stirred with purpose.

The storm had passed.

But the dawn was only beginning.